The Broken Cedar

Also by Martin Malone

Us

After Kafra

MARTIN MALONE

The Broken Cedar

Scribner

First published in Great Britain by Scribner, 2003
An imprint of Simon & Schuster UK Ltd
A Viacom Company

1 3 5 7 9 10 8 6 4 2

Simon & Schuster UK Ltd
Africa House
64–78 Kingsway
London WC2B 6AH

Simon & Schuster Australia
Sydney

www.simonsays.co.uk

A CIP catalogue record for this book is available
from the British Library

ISBN 0-7432-3170-8

Typeset by M Rules
Printed and bound in Great Britain by
The Bath Press, Bath

Acknowledgements

I'd like to thank Faith O'Grady, Seamus Hosey, The Arts Council of Ireland, and all at Scribner UK for their support and encouragement. I'd also like to thank my wife Bernadette, and sons, Colin and Barry, for the sacrifices they made so this book could be written.

Khalil would say, 'Shukran'.

Murt

They cannot scare me with their empty spaces
Between stars – on stars where no human race is.
I have it in me so much nearer home
To scare myself with my own desert places.

Robert Frost, an extract from his poem, *Desert Places*.

Part I

1

South Lebanon, 6 km from the Israeli border, 1994.

The one-sided street meanders snakelike, fracturing in three places – at its northern tail beyond the French Wadi Gate where the road slims to meet a tight bend before the port, midway when the road shoots up a long broad and twisting way to the hilltop village, and at its southern out-reaches where the bulk of the shops squat, leaving behind the disused whorehouse, a half-built hotel and a dump smoking its own filth. The pockmarked asphalt yawns to Roshaniqra Border Crossing. Sea winds snatch at the Star of David flag on its mast above the customs offices. Beneath the post, winds sail into the sea caves and turning about at speed scale the chalk cliffs, passing bent and rusted railway tracks.

The old man sleeps in the back room of his shop near the

French Wadi Gate. With him sleeps the gnawing pain that shows in occasional flinches about the corners of his eyes – physical pain and something deeper, more spiritual, a truth that festers. There is no respite for him. Tortured – morning, noon and night by something growing within him. There is that – the cancer blackening his innards. And there is the harbouring of a secret, the last surviving member of a group that corked the truth with their tongues. These days he feels as though his soul and heart are bound by tightening vines. When the day is young he will think of these things – things he has thought of before and often.

Khalil Abbas awakens to the call of the muezzin, a lonely lament descending from the village's minaret, combing the scrub covered slopes that are scarred with goat trails – the ink staining the skies beginning to clear. He turns over on the mattress, careful not to disturb the phlegm still at rest in his lungs and yet needing to answer his throat's whisper for thick coffee and his bladder's cry for relief.

The wind howls. Moves along the tin roof, tearing at its edges, pushing against the door, trembling through a fissure in the window, stirring curtains he seldom draws against the night. Sometimes the stars hold his gaze.

He arrived here sixteen years ago, fleeing Beirut before the civil war worsened. Muslim and Christian at each other's throats. The Palestinians carried their war to Israel from Lebanon, eventually causing the Israelis to invade Lebanon in 1978 and again in 1982. Khalil had always empathized with the Palestinians, shut away as they were in refugee camps outside Beirut, Sidon, Tyre, and in Jordan, disenfranchised of their homes, land and country – forced into exile in the late 1940s by the Jews who wanted their own state and took it.

Palestinians cling to worthless bonds and deeds for properties that now belong to someone else. Yes, Khalil understands, and understands too that for Lebanon to become a nation again the Palestinians must remain policed. For the Palestinian conflict brought in the invader and great destruction and loss of life. Jews and their Christian allies fought against the majority Muslim population. Cousins – the Jew and Arab – ah, family wars are the worst of wars.

And yet, these days, with the Palestinians pigeon-holed in their camps and guarded by the reformed Lebanese army, the war continues, with the Hezbollah vowing not to quit until Israel withdraws to the Internationally Recognized Frontier. Always a reason for war. Always a war.

Early on a dry and crisp Sunday morning in Beirut as he cleaned his electrical shop in Rue Dunant, a thriving business on an upward curve, the patisserie two doors away was sprayed with machine-gun fire from a neighbour's balcony. If this were Christian fire Khalil would have not have been shocked, but Muslim shot at Muslim in order to extort money. Enemies all round – No . . . No . . . No!

He brought his family to Sidon, about 45 km south of Beirut, staying in an apartment that overlooked the crusader sea castle, near the vibrant fishing port, but they weren't safe there either.

Militias roamed the streets, vying for power, looting, setting up checkpoints, every night there was a shooting. Sometimes gun battles raged during the day – anarchy – jackals fighting over bones and Israeli warplanes lacerating the city and its districts. On a quiet Saturday morning he loaded the pick-up and moved farther south, bypassing Tyre, crossing over the unofficial border the Israelis manufactured to keep their northern territories safe from guerrilla attack. A buffer zone or as he had come to know it, *The Enclave*. Building a home cum shop of tin and wood alongside others sprouting up to service the needs of UN, United Nations, troops stationed in barracks behind the giant T walls paralleling the length of the fledgling shanty town.

A dissonance of foreign voices – Irish, Dutch, Fijian, Polish, Nepalese, Finns, Ghanaians and Norwegians – the street alive at night, the restaurants full and songs and arguments fading as curfew fell at eleven – the soldiers draining away through the blue doors that the French controlled. Metal doors that shut with a clanging noise signalling Khalil's own bedtime. He was forty-eight years old back then. Thin, tall, balding, a wart flanking his nose, large green eyes. Quiet when others insisted on talking, slow to react when others demanded action – revenge, violence, always something bloody, demanding the sort of action that appalled him. Israel – the Palestinians, revenge – as though revenge would replace those and that lost. Don't they see that the letting of blood becomes as wearisome as listening to the rhetoric of firebrand imams and western propaganda? He speaks now with the wisdom of one living within sight of his own grave.

He eases his feet into flip-flops, pads outside and pisses against the rippled wall of his shop, the stench rising to greet his nostrils a solution of medications intended to break up the phlegm and assist with his breathing.

The medications give him hope.

The heart attack three years ago in the spring of 1991 started it, the slide. The searing pain, the time spent in Marjayoun Hospital, thinking how dramatically a few seconds can change a man's life. An energetic bustling trader reduced to a mass of quivering fear and a dread of another bolt, more alive to his own mortality than ever before, rubbing his father's prayer beads between pads of thumb and forefinger till the beads had a shine that outdid his father's.

He dips his hand into a blue basin with its rim broken in places and takes in the cracked mirror, the lines about his eyes like curtain pleats, the yellow in the whites of them signifying the poison swimming through his veins.

He shaves slowly, each dip of the blade sullies the water with dabs of foam flecked with stubble.

The wind has not let up and he knows of old that it will blow for another day at least. Early spring and he feels the chill of a bad winter in his bones. He looks forward to the summer as the sun paints a better picture of things. It lies. Next winter? His eyes don't tell him. It is because they are blind to the future. Caused by an acceptance of his lot?

He hears the boy from next door singing. He is Dahab's son, her surviving boy. About eight years old he is always first up in the morning.

The song the boy sings won the Eurovision contest last night – 'Rock and Roll Boys'. Khalil had watched it on TV in the shop with three Irish military policemen who had just arrived in Lebanon to begin a six months tour of duty. He knew two of them from other trips and one he did not know; though he said he had been in Lebanon before.

'When?'

'Ninety-two – I was in Irishbatt – I was here, in your shop before, a flying visit.'

'I see – Tibnin, the mountains, yes – with the Headquarters MPs now?'

'Yes and no – I am working on something else.'

Khalil frowned. The other had neither offered nor asked for a name. No smile roosted on his lean hard face, his hair as dark as night, his eyes cold and blue with a piercing intensity that logged all he saw. For some reason Khalil had not warmed to him and this in itself was unusual for he was a warm man. To make a point Khalil handed him a tin of cola and studied his name tag. The name in black letters, stitching frayed in a corner, threw him. He recovered quickly, nodded. Hurried a frozen smile to his lips.

'Driscoll – O'Driscoll – Sergeant O'Driscoll – yes?'

'Yes.'

The sergeant shook hands and then took the proffered cola and untabbed the ring, 'Thanks.'

The MPs, Military Police, were good to know. They had helped him before on many occasions to track down default-ers – UN soldiers to whom he had given items on credit.

Usually a word with an MP saw the soldier arrive within a day or so to clear the bill.

He calls the boy. He comes running to the back door and stands there for moments looking in. Short trousers, white T-shirt with a Hard Rock Café Beirut logo, plastic sandals.

'Coffee, Daoud?'

The boy nods. Rakes his fingers through short matted hair the colour of cedar bark.

Daoud smiles. Khalil sees the boy's older brother in that smile and something gives in his heart – like a sensation of falling.

'Yes, Khalil. Or coke, you have coke?'

'It's too early for coke. Would your mother give you coke at this hour?'

Daoud shakes his head and then moves to the armchair and sits down. He is a small boy for his age – like his country he has seen much – much violence in the home, and muffled and strangled cries behind the curtains dividing the sleeping spaces. It is good that Aziz has gone to live in his new house in the village with his new wife. Beatings are easy to tolerate when divided between wives – this is what Dahab says.

'You watched the song contest last night, Khalil?'

Nods.

'You like the Irish song?'

'Aha – yes, very good. My mother says the Irish are the best at making music.'

'Probably, probably this is true.'

'I think the Americans are – they make the best movies anyway.'

Khalil makes coffee in a small pot and pours it thick and brown, rich in grits, into miniature cups. Hands one to Daoud.

They nibble at pitta bread. The boy is a noisy eater, his tongue foraging along his lips for escapee crumbs. Khalil had felt hungry but the hunger has given way to the nausea he expected but had prayed against – his appetite plays tricks all the time.

His body's rejection of food is telling him something. He doesn't want to hear but his body screams. It screams at him in the smell of his piss, the belly cramps, and an invisible hunger. The bile it throws into his mouth leaves a sour taste to suppress the one of mouthwash.

Some of his clients know – his worn and haggard appearance an open book. Especially soldiers, they know, understand immediately at first sight when they return after a year or six months absence that the Khalil of their photos and memories is not the Khalil they know.

Inshallah he says to them and to himself, smiling and moving away from the silent topic. He wants to tell them nothing and he understands that they don't really want to hear. What else should he do? Whine? Moan about his fate? Isn't he lucky to have grown old? They remembered him from a time when a smile sat on his face as easily as the sun sat in the sky. Best to leave them with that memory, a smile, even if contrived.

All he has to do is wait and enjoy as much as possible whatever time he has left.

There is no good in airing the poison in him – what good will it do fifteen years on to dredge up the past? He is certain that O'Driscoll has returned to Lebanon to turn back the pages of time.

Zarifa will be here tomorrow, from Beirut, from seeing a specialist about the angry veins in the back of her legs, from seeing Adeeba, their only daughter, who married a pig gen-darme, a man who whistles at traffic from under his mushroom shelter and later returns home to beat his wife. She will also carry results of his latest tests – tests he reluc-tantly underwent to appease Zarifa – by consultants in a private hospital, people skilful enough to add ten years to a man's life, or so Zarifa believed and tried to have him believe too.

2

He shuffles through his shop to the front door, Daoud in close attendance. Draws the brass bolts from the door, the last one, ankle high, always stiff. There are scuff marks on the grey paint from the constant placing there of his foot.

'Wake up, Daoud – when I push against the door free the bolt.'

Daoud drops to his hunkers, features shading to serious – it's good to make a child feel important.

He stands outside, under the canopy, taking in the morning, a yellow air of dust and wind. He squints, holds a face towel to the small cyst under his right eye and walks slowly to Dahab's. The boy remains in the shop, watching cartoons on TV. Feeling important. Needed. Yes, Khalil, of course I will sweep the floor, he grinned, chill out. Khalil turns the advice over in his mind, 'Chill out.' Indeed!

Dahab is up. Already the ironing board is raised and the iron plugged in. To make some extra money she takes in clothes to wash and iron from the Irish and Norwegians. He doesn't have much time for Aziz and Dahab. Always had a reserve towards them since they forced their son into joining the Israeli militia, and for how they revealed no guilt over his death, the way the boy turned his own rifle on himself. He sees them sometimes making their way into the UN camp, to the cemetery near the sea, burning mint leaves for their boy.

Dahab breathes of bully NCOs, non-commissioned officers, in the militia and of the sights her son saw in the compounds, the attacks from the Hezbollah – it is true when people say someone was blown out of his boots and that human flesh in a bombed car smells like burning pork. It is easy for Dahab to say these things, because surely such scenes would drive anyone mad – look what happened to Sami?

She forgets that Khalil is next door and that he remembers nights when she and Aziz pleaded with Sami to join the militia.

'Think of it – I can travel into Israel to work,' Dahab said.

'We can have free hospital services – Daoud will be able to attend a private school,' Aziz said.

Coaxing and shouting at Sami after he said, 'No.' Hitting

14

him with prolonged periods of stony silence, making up then, fussing over him, afterwards saying softly that Daoud needed a serious operation, leaving the news to sink in, the lie to ferment. Khalil regretted that he had not advised the boy, handed him a few dollars to get away somewhere. But family matters . . .

It is why he befriended Daoud – always he tells him to be strong, always he talks to him of other places. He allows the boy to sit with him some evenings when he has visitors from the camp. They ask sometimes if Daoud is his grandson and he smiles and says, 'More than a grandson.'

It is something for them to talk about. His son? Dirty old man.

Dahab says, her voice a lifeless monotone, that his clothes are ready. She is a small woman, petite, with skin a tint darker than olive. Dahab keeps her long brown hair under her scarf. She is younger, he suspects, than her actual age. A mystery to him given her hard life – it might have something to do with her ability to distance herself from truth. He reproaches himself – had he not done, is he not doing, the same?

'Daoud is minding the shop?' She smiles thinly.

'Yes, he is – he will sweep the floor after the cartoons.'

She nods.

'You don't mind. It is good to have a young boy in the house. So active – brings back memories of Adeeba when she was small.'

'No, no – not at all – perhaps he will pick up some wisdom.'

'Inshallah,' breathes Khalil, showing some pleasure at the flattery.

'He will learn none from Aziz, that is for sure.'

He feels her pain. The new wife lodges in the new house while she and Daoud live in a shack. Aziz was here last night, she says.

Yes. He had heard. Heard his Mercedes pull up outside, his call, her telling him to leave and he laughing it off as a joke, taking her later that night, not so much against her will as she would like Khalil to believe, but against her will nevertheless. After all, if she didn't concur with his wishes he would rant and throw things around, upsetting Daoud. Better to demur, kick up a little but not much fuss. Comply with just a little defiance. She asked if his new wife – never called her by name – was unwell, unable to satisfy him. He said it was good to change the bed.

He takes the bundle of clothes she indicates and leaves $3 on the table. Neither she nor he ever mentions money. He had asked her to take over doing his laundry because Zarifa's finger joints ached badly. He knew she needed the money and at that time she hadn't much business. She was too proud to accept charity. Zarifa complained a little, suspected him of having an affair, but gradually let it go – it was a charitable deed on her husband's part. No more. Zarifa says she would sooner die than have another woman wash her clothes. It is just a 'thing' with her. Personal. Worth a little finger pain. Pushed a little by Khalil to explain her 'thing' she said she wouldn't have that woman talking about her behind her back, telling people that she had taken on airs and graces.

He pauses outside Dahab's and indulges in discourse with Kasni, the militia chief, on his way to the tailor's beside Dahab's. He is a short balding man with a thick moustache, a revolver encased in a leather holster on his hip, partially hidden by his sleeveless jacket. The man is a distant cousin. Khalil had heard rumours of his harsh treatment of prisoners in Khiam Prison. Still, you would not think it to look at him. Mild-mannered and polite, on his way to be measured for a suit for his sister's wedding – you'll be there, Khalil – you and Zarifa?

There are invitations you don't decline.

Zarifa is right. The business has fallen away. It shows in the boarded up shacks that run from his shop to the UN Gate. The soldiers are fewer in number these days, thousands fewer. The troops spend their money on gold and in restaurants. Mostly, they travel to Tyre or Beirut to shop. During the civil war it was different – travel was restricted and they bought in shops like his.

Costs had risen so much that there wasn't much difference in price between his shop and a shop in a soldier's home country. And after all, he could not provide him with an after sales service.

He survived by offering credit terms and becoming extra friendly with the troops, talking at length with them, offering teas and colas with the knowledge that they would, at some point, check out his stock and perhaps buy something.

In the old days he did a lot of business with the Irish, but they bought little from him now, knowing where to buy better a little cheaper. It is the business way. Those with whom he deals he barters with, knowing they will give in and buy from him. But the Ghanaians and Nepalese don't know when to quit. They haggle him beyond his profit margin and he lightly beats his chest and shakes his head and says,

'I cannot sell you this – for me no money – I buy from the man that price and I sell you this price – you see what I make – see my fingers. Four dollars – no more. I swear to you the truth, my friend. You don't believe me – check my books, come check my books.'

They never do.

Back in the shop he pumps the heater with kerosene and sets a lighter to its wick. The globe's mesh wires creak as they redden. Zarifa prefers to fill the small brazier with charcoal and sit around it at night with him, warming pieces of pitta bread for a few seconds on the smoking coals before eating them. She spends most nights in their house in the village. Many of the Street's traders had built fine homes in the village on the hill. A few like him prefer to live in their shops. It is as though they owe the shacks something for having provided them with such luxuries they assumed had been lost to them forever. Khalil also understands that before the UN arrived there was no Mingi Street and in time the Street will be no more. Zarifa is at him lately to close the shop, to turn the key and walk away.

How can she expect it of him?

'You are sixty-four, Khalil, not a young man any more.' She speaks with a dialect he loves.

He was introduced to her, a native of Baalbek in the Bekaa Valley, by a friend. As pleasing to the eye as spring flowers growing wild on mountain flanks. Now she was bending with the weight of the years, her features thickly lined about the eyes and lips. She detested living on the Street and the house he built had at the time unburdened her of much. Zarifa feared the Israeli half-tracks as they roared along the street, the cars driven by young people who had little choice of road to travel as they raced up and down the one out front. She told him the shop wasn't doing the business it used to, failing to realize that that wasn't the reason he continued to ply his wares. What would he do in the village? Sit out and watch the dogs shade themselves from the sun, he thought one evening, as they drank black sugary tea after she had started with her antics about him retiring.

Daoud is busy sweeping the floor at the end of the shop. But Khalil notices that the cleanest part of the concrete floor is that in front of the TV. At least the boy had showed initiative in moving before his boss returned. It is important to let him know though that bosses aren't stupid. Or at least they shouldn't be.

'Watching TV and working when I was at your mother's. Was it not hard for you to do these two things at once?'

Daoud smiles. Lowers his head. Shy. No denial from him. Good, very good.

He tells the boy to come sit by the fire.

'It's pay day – isn't it, Daoud?'

Nods.

'Due an increase are you?'

Shakes his head.

'I don't want money any more, Khalil.'

'No?'

'Will you keep my money until I have enough to buy a G Shock?'

'A watch – you're sure?'

'Yes.'

'What watch?' Khalil points to a shelf of them on window display.

The boy brushes past Khalil and picks up a green G Shock – expensive, much too wide for his thin wrist. Still . . .

'Daoud, do you know how much this is?'

'Yes. One hundred dollars.'

'Ninety for my staff.'

Daoud's smile is uncertain. It grieves Khalil to see a child suspicious at a kindness. He realizes it is from having a shortage of small kindnesses in his young life.

'But at two dollars a week, Daoud—'

'I don't mind waiting.'

'O.K. I'll put it aside for you – write your name on the price tag.'

Daoud's eyes moisten with a joy he finds hard to contain. 'Aw right! Thanks, Khalil.'

Sounds American. Khalil resists the temptation to say, 'Chill out.'

When he is gone Khalil weighs the watch in his hand. Green, luminous light, works underwater. Robust, ideal for a robust boy – interesting to see how long his resolve to earn it lasts. He cleans dust from the watch with a cloth and then consigns it to his desk drawer. A kept dream.

3

The hunger comes at him. It is a dual hunger – one of an uncompromising urge to divulge a secret and the other to eat a substantial meal. The latter would make him sick and the former – ach . . . think about other things. Come, you are well practised at distracting yourself.

Focuses his eyes on the shop's Perspex windows, behind which he keeps shelves of watches, silver trinkets, lighters, Swiss army knives, small diversifications from his range of electrical goods – battery toothbrushes, CD players, irons, kettles, Casio and Cannon typewriters, lamps, radios, portable TVs, sandwich makers. In a room off the main shop floor, up three steps of worn and blackened timber, there are shelves and a mid floor table capped with crockery, cutlery, Damascus tablecloths, Christmas tree lights and other bric-a-brac, the majority of items for practical everyday use. Briefly he considers covering them from the pervasive yellow dust but decides not to bother as the dust of time is on them anyway.

He buys his goods from Beirut some 120 km away to the north. Smuggled goods in the main but his sources are drying up, moving on to improved things. And smuggling isn't so easy since the war ended. Lebanon now has a government, an army and a newly found desire to pull itself out of the gutter. Here, in *The Enclave*, controlled by the Israelis and their puppet army, the SLA, South Lebanese Army, smuggling is ongoing, mostly in the lines of alcohol and cigarettes. He hears that a bottle of Chivas Regal sells for almost three times its Beirut price. Customs officers spring checkpoints on the bridge at the Litani river outside Tyre and in Sidon and Beirut but they don't stop the UN drivers. It is a way to move things. Unifil – the United Nations Interim Force in Lebanon – is aware of what's going on. Their MPs on detachment carry out spot checks but the manpower isn't there to be effective and besides the corruption is rife, comes from deep within and flows from the top to the bottom. He knows these things because he listens, has always listened – slow to react, always too slow to react. Afraid of doing something wrong, saying the wrong word, giving a wrong look – for any of these things on its own is enough to earn a bullet, to disappear. The danger is not so real these days as it was during the civil war when life meant nothing – when whole families were wiped out. There were those who used the war to their own benefit, settling old scores that might not have been much more than slights with an unanswerable bullet.

Cold. He wears a long one-piece garment, blue and white vertical stripes, loose fitting. The wind unsettles him, the way it carries the dust and speaks in howls, moans and whispers. An atavistic chill inches along his spine, filling the pit of his stomach with an iciness, as though a freezer bag had burst in his gut.

In time his shop will be like the others, boarded up with thick planks, tumbleweed snagged against the door, the shelves bare, the smell of kerosene and charcoal long dissi-pated, the haw of his breath no more. He will be in the cemetery by the sea, with mint leaves smoking over him and tears moistening the scarlet anemones Zarifa will place in vases above his head. At least, at least she will have a grave to grieve over – in another land there is a woman who has none.

He slips on his long black coat and a blue scarf Adeeba had bought him for his birthday, but the chill remains. Rabin is on TV, pledging that Israel will respond in due course to the Katyusha rocket attacks on Qiryat Shemona last night. He creams his lips to prevent them cracking, and drinks some cola to moisten a dry tongue. Outside the wind plays up and down the street.

He knows them all on the street, their petty jealousies, the ones who had come and gone, the ones who had died and like him were dying. Atab the gay hairstylist ordered out of Sidon by the Hezbollah who hadn't taken to his pink string vests and claret short shorts. Jesso the ex-commando who sells booze and cigarettes to the messes and turns dollars into shekels and back again. Tommy the Coffee Man who peddles coffee from his van. Porno Joe who sells filth from his X Shop. Ali Strawballs and his *Best* gold shop. Rose Najm and Samia Haqqi who manage the street's sole hotel across from Le Moulin Rouge, the deserted former brothel. Yazbek Sharif who runs the Clara Shop. Salam Zoroob the Twilight hotel, Alma Ash another gold shop, Bassam Kostantine's Elsa Video Shop, Josef Shoabiye's Ramada Restaurant, Tom Cruise the Laundry Man, Pablo and his bar with the only draught beer in Mingi Street. Mansur the Tailor with his one arm. Adnan's Splash Restaurant, Rafi Sasin's Garfield Shop, Atwi's Golden Fish restaurant – he knows them all – some by their real names and others by those accorded to them by the UN troops. He had alliances with them at the beginning, when each helped the other, at a time before they realized that they were eating from the same cake and small and large rivalries didn't exist. It all changed. One watched what the other got and did. The more successful you became the less popular you were among the other traders. He was always middle of the road popular.

It was the Irish who named the shanty town 'Mingi Street'. A man called Dawson said the Irish learned the word in the Congo, and it meant a cheap present of dubious quality, and the seller of such wares was known as a Mingi Man.

Fake Lacoste, fake Levis, fake just about everything. It is true and there is no real problem with that. The problems start when the fake costs as much as if not more than the genuine and soldiers discover they have been cheated. These days, reflects Khalil, like so much else in the world, it is hard to tell which is real and which isn't, who lies and who doesn't.

Dawson lost his smile when Khalil asked if he thought he was a poor quality man – isn't that what Mingi means? You've just told me – believe me, my friend, I am not. Then he smiled. He always smiled.

He closes the shop early and draws the curtains so no one passing will see him through the shop windows. The yellow dust storm has lasted all day and as night falls, and it falls quickly, he hears the distant rumble of thunder and knows it is on the march, heading this way from the sea.

Opening the back door he spits into the night, onto a rainwater puddle lit by flash lightning. Emptying his lungs of phlegm in the knowledge that before he is settled in bed they will refill and the spittoon by his side will not remain idle.

He moves in the heater from the shop and fills Zarifa's hot water bottle. She always says that he should use an electric blanket, but no – he fears fire, fears burning. After taking his medication he slips under the duvets. His bed a mattress on a Persian rug his father bought in Baghdad from a Kurd on the banks of the Tigris.

He lies on his back, taking in the red orange wires, the lightning when it flashes silvery on the concrete floor. Listening to the rapid dancing of raindrops on the tin roof, the soft drip coming from a spot where it always leaks, landing in a basin in which he had placed a towel to deaden the noise.

The storm rages for most of the night. He is alive to his thoughts and his pain. Sleep shies from him like a nervous camel – doesn't sleep until after the call to prayer from the minaret. The thunder had rolled to distant wadis and hills. Fading voices. The morning songbirds silent.

The knock is loud and persistent. Milliseconds for the fugue in his head to clear and determine the source. Daoud? Bleary eyed he eases from bed and shuffles for the door, settling his sandals on his feet as he walks, adjusting his dress.

The light is strong on his eyes, forcing him to squint. Not Daoud.

'Zarifa! You are here early.'

He stands aside to let her pass. The scent of her perfume is rich, her eyes shadowed with blue liner, her hair groomed

but not freshly cut. He knows she has bought things for
herself that he will not see until she is sure he is in the right
mood to admire them and not query the expense.

'Such a time of it,' she says, bustling by him.

Her coat smells of rain.

'The traffic in Beirut is terrible – getting worse each time
I visit – why can't it be more like Paris or London – organized. The gendarmes make up their own rules – one day a
street is one way, the next it is not.'

He nods, feels his stubble, wishing he had woken earlier
and shaved. She speaks of the weather in Beirut, the cold,
the wet and muddy streets, the buildings coming down, the
ones going up, and of Adeeba who is at home in the village.
After saying this she awaits his response.

'For a visit?' he says.

'Longer.'

He says nothing. He supposes Adeeba will help in the
shop. She likes to do that – used to like doing that. He lights
the stove and puts on a pot of water to brew coffee. Zarifa
removes her coat and pegs it to a hook, rubs her hands in
front of the heater.

'Your legs?' he says.

'I need an operation on the veins – yes, an operation.'

'Adeeba – that pig of hers?'

'He doesn't mind her staying. I told him she was needed to
run the shop. He put a face on him. You know his face?' She

lifts her nostrils with her thumb, 'But smiled when I said Adeeba will be paid for her troubles.'

'Run the shop?' Khalil says quietly.

Two birds with one stone – her family under the one roof again.

Zarifa is a clever woman. He nods, turns his back to her and steps onto the shop floor, scene of many deals and clasped hands. He kills the tears in his eyes with a blink. Zarifa puts her hand on his shoulder and he rests his on top, his palm pressing down on her ring. Her voice coos in his ear, her words gentle but telling, 'It's time.'

He sighs. His throat strangled with the news she has broken without saying a word about the results of his test – yes, it is time, and perhaps he should try to amend the sin on his soul before it is finally too late.

But would it not be considered a worse sin to tell? Surely, the time has come and gone for the truth to see daylight?

Voice!

Is the decision to reveal the secret yours and yours alone to make?

4

Zarifa hands him the keys to their Mercedes Benz. A lime green car with scrapes and dents on its flanks. He bought it in Tyre last year, had driven into the Sidonian harbour and watched the cars leaving the Cypriot ship, choosing the Merc after a detailed inspection on the docks. Paid cash, $7,000, and handed the keys of his old car to a young soldier who still probably squeezed his beret and wondered where was the catch.

After the deal was done he had said to his friend Brahim Sourb, an official of Amal, one of the main political parties in Free Lebanon, that these latest cars would see them out. They smiled – continued on their way to the port on the Christian Maronite side – not realizing then how true Khalil's small joke would prove.

The cars come from Europe – Germany and Denmark.

You can buy top of the range models for a quarter of what it would cost in a European country. But like everything else in Free Lebanon costs are shooting up – the price of peace.

They parked their new second-hand cars outside Café Soueidan in Rue Abu Dib and ate a lunch of *kibbe*, ground lamb and cracked wheat croquettes stuffed with a savoury meat filling.

They sat indoors by the window, preferring the air conditioning to the outdoor veranda where the flies were eager to share in the meal. Across the narrow road tourists entered the Roman Hippodrome and walked the flagged Roman way that had once been the main route into the city. As a boy he had run his fingers along the chariot ruts and looked in at the bones in the sarcophagi in the Byzantine cemetery that sprays from the Roman archway – a cemetery known as the City of the Dead. Ornate tombs carried reliefs and inscriptions and he had asked his father what they meant. His father shrugged and said it didn't matter what they meant, that it was the living who mattered – the dead were dead and you couldn't help them. That he was a boy who thought too much.

Most of Tyre's antiquities had been buried during the war or taken to the museum in Beirut and placed in underground vaults. In spite of these precautions much smuggling had occurred. You can get away with murder during war, his father used to say – it took Khalil a while to realize that his father was being cryptic.

Brahim breathed some queries about Zarifa's and Adeeba's wellbeing until interrupted by the sound of tank fire from Charlie Swing Gate, an SLA position on the Naqoura road, marking the border between what Brahim called Free and Occupied Lebanon.

'Their days are numbered,' Brahim said of the SLA.

He was tall and lean with a shock of snow-white hair he had swept back, revealing a widow's peak. He wore a short-sleeved cream shirt and grey Farah slacks, black leather sandals. Blue prayer beads in his left hand. Coughed often the cough Khalil now coughs.

'Do you think so?'

'Of course – the Israelis are losing too many of their soldiers – our boys and the Hezbollah are teaching them a lesson.'

'It is hard to imagine them leaving – what will become of the SLA?'

Shrugged. Sipped at his coffee, patted his breast pocket for cigarettes and seeing them on the table lit up. Khalil too. They were full after the meal, content in themselves – a new car and lunch with an old friend – the sun up, red flowers dancing on grass embankments that for short distances obscured their view of the Hippodrome. The only blight on their mood was the sound of distant tank fire – always war in the background of their lives, the noise of it, the effects of it. Always. The sound of distant gunfire never distant enough.

Brahim exhaled cigarette smoke, slid back his chair and crossed his long legs. Waved his cigarette as though it were a conductor's wand.

'Do you know why we will win and they will lose?'

'Win, lose – there'll be a winner?'

'Our resistance fighters are not afraid to die – the Israelis are – their bellies are soft. They are not like the old Israeli warriors. They wouldn't have gone on patrol with mobile phones that ring and alert an enemy to their position. They would not have pursued an enemy and used up all their ammunition – our fighters turning around then to shoot them dead like they would dogs. And Israeli mothers are lobbying support for Rabin to withdraw their boys – see, everyone knows they shouldn't be here – their soldiers don't have the stomach for the fight. And they have no right to be here. It is not their land.'

'I cannot see them abandoning the SLA.'

'Wait. Watch. Five or six years, a little longer – you'll see.'

'Unifil?'

'They'll leave when we want them to.'

'The Syrians, too?'

Brahim fanned smoke from his eyes with his hand, 'That, I can't answer.'

After a silence of about a minute Brahim said, 'We have

done well to reach our respective ages, Khalil, given what we lived through, what we've seen happen to our country and its people, things that could easily have happened to us, my old friend. Allah is kind. We had His blessings.'

Khalil resented the other's slight show of smugness. He found it distasteful without knowing why. After all what Brahim said was true. They were indeed fortunate.

Khalil asked about the *night*. He wanted to know if his friend's conscience troubled him as much as his own. A guilt spoken of was a guilt halved? No.

Brahim stirred uneasily on his wicker chair and freshened their glasses with coffee. He sucked in his cheeks, leaned his head back as though he had caught an unexpected odour. Had he a store of bad memories? Similar to or worse than those of the *night*.

'Best forgotten as we agreed back then, Khalil – what good comes of it to raise this matter?'

'He is not at rest.'

'At rest? Who cares? Me? You? I don't. Why do you?'

'He—'

'Was a fool.'

'Human. He was human, too.'

Brahim leaned forward. Khalil saw the liver spots through his snowy hair, the glint of annoyance in his brown eyes. He did not like the dead being raised – not unless the dead was an Amal martyr.

'If you cared so much then why didn't you object that night? Why didn't you come forward and shout, "Stop!"?'

Khalil had no answer.

'There were not so many of us that you couldn't have intervened – isn't that so?'

Khalil sighed and tamped his cigarette in a green Heineken ashtray. The air had turned cool. Fanned so by awkward questions that probed to the bone – questions he had asked himself for years.

Brahim got to his feet, stuffed his cigarette pack and lighter in his pocket, towered over Khalil, his finger a warning stick, 'Forget him, forget that night, forget what happened – as we promised each other – not a word to another soul. Never.'

'Never? We must answer to Allah. Mustn't we?'

'Not till then.'

Brahim spread some Lebanese pounds on the table, tapped his watch with his forefinger and said he had to go. See you again, soon – inshallah.

Khalil didn't move for some minutes. When he did it was to order another coffee. There was no sense in heading for Mingi Street, as he wouldn't get past Charlie Swing Gate until its Sherman tank had fallen quiet.

He watched his friend's new black tyres turn the dust under them into clouds. A few months later Brahim died from a heart attack. He had been attending the opening of a mosque on a hillside outside Jezzine. His widow said that it was evening time and a full moon had been rising from behind an outcrop of rock. They were admiring its beauty, wondering at how close it appeared to be – when it happened.

Now, Khalil walks outside to the car, sees a fresh dent, souvenir from Beirut, and sighs. Women! So concerned about cosmetics yet thinking nothing about a car's. Zarifa will mind the shop for him for a few hours, give it a good cleaning, and Allah help the poor soldier who wanders in as the floor is drying. A sharp look and the birth of a certain atmosphere will send him on his way.

The midmorning air is clear, the skies blue, the weather still and settled. A quiet day.

Daoud sits outside with his feet on the small concrete divide, between his home and Khalil's shop, that used to hold a trellis of honeysuckle. He's eating cornflakes with a plastic spoon, reading a comic.

'*Marhaba*, Khalil.'

'*Ahlan beek*.'

Khalil turns the ignition and eases into the short drive to the village. The house is two storeyed with a spacious interior. A red pantiled roof always reminds him of a roof he had seen in a storybook his father had bought for him in Tripoli on his seventh birthday – a story about Marco Polo and his travels.

The house has fine marble floors and columns and elegant bathrooms in three of its four bedrooms. A basement holds a games room and emergency supplies for the bunker it might become if the war between the Hezbollah and the Israelis escalates.

There is always a danger of things escalating in Lebanon.

It was built piecemeal and relatively cheaply from materials siphoned from the UN camp and labour brought in from poorer villages. In all his wildest dreams he had never contemplated owning such a house. His father would have been proud if a little perturbed at the style and extravagance. Ostentatious – the very reason he prefers to live in the shop. To live in a house like this a person has to throw a little sand over his conscience and shade his eyes to the stark truths of the homeless.

He brakes sedately alongside the kerb, cuts the engine and alights, stays by the car a few moments because the pain has come at him, sharp and prolonged, like a knife slicing between his ribs. He sits back in the car and takes his pills from the glove compartment, swallows them with quick gulps from a bottle of water. After the battle he pads beyond the wrought-iron gates into his garden – olive trees and sunflowers and a variety of shrubs Zarifa likes to name off in his presence in the same way and with the same attention to detail that he would list his stock.

The times he likes best in this house are after a hot shower in the evening. Relaxed. Sitting in the garden with the plants freshly watered, their scents playing on the air – a glass of arrack in his hand, the bottle close by. A cigar going, or the water pipe bubbling – though he seldom smokes hash these days and when he does he prefers to roll a cigarette.

Entering the kitchen he hears music – Fairouz on Lebanese radio singing '*Bayaa al Khawatem*', the seller of rings – a long time since he heard her singing that particular song. When Beirut was reunified he was among the 40,000 who crammed into the Place des Martyrs in the ravaged downtown district to hear her perform. What a weekend! Magical – an Aladdin's cave of treasures, love awakened by the sweep of old songs to their ears.

Staying in the Lord's Hotel, shopping in Rue Hamra, he and Zarifa – walking the Corniche, eating falafels as they took in the Pigeon's Grotto, an unusual rock formation jutting up from the sea a stone's throw from the shore. Ah, maybe once more? If time allows – or is it best to leave Zarifa with the memory of a perfect three days? Why sully it by giving her a memory of an ailing old man trying to pretend nothing was wrong? No.

Adeeba smiles when she sees him. Not quickly enough to hide her momentary surprise at his condition.

That bad?

'Father.'

Still, the old reserve – the wary look.

'Adeeba.'

Embers of bruising under her left eye.

'It's over?' he says.

Nods.

'He married someone else?'

'Yes.'

'Is divorcing you?'

'Yes.'

'So he will have two wives instead of three – measuring his cloth at last.'

How old is she? Thirty-seven? She has had three stillborn children, more miscarriages, and the pain of unfulfilled motherhood shows in her eyes. Adeeba's fingers are devoid of rings. She moves about the kitchen fussing over nothings. She is thin and pale, fretful. Fine lines map the corners of her green eyes and although her features are pretty she has above her lips the fine downy hair of a youth's first stubble. The butt of Ossie's cruel jokes, he expects, the reason her hand goes to her face when she speaks. Not to stop lies spilling from her mouth but to shield herself from critical comments. She wears jeans and a mauve T-shirt that is loose and unironed, fresh from the suitcase.

'Who told you it was over? Mother?'

'No one. I knew.'

She rakes her short dark hair and sits down at the table, in front of an iced tea. He pours some pomegranate juice from the fridge and sits beside her. She touches his hand and draws away.

'I'm sorry.'

'For what?'

'Providing you with no grandchildren – you always wanted a son, a boy . . .'

He says nothing for this is true and to lie now is to pander to her – she would resent him for it.

'I have had worse disappointments in life. I was gifted with a beautiful daughter – I am well satisfied with that.'

Her eyes moisten.

'Ossie would sometimes look at me and say you had a son.'

'It is easier for weak men to be cruel rather than kind. Necessary for them.'

A sigh escapes her.

'You will find someone else.'

'I'm not looking to find anyone else – I'm thirty-eight years old, Father, don't patronize me. You're being kind, I know, but—'

'I understand.'

Later, from the back garden he sees the length of Mingi Street, the horizon, the apartment towers of Tyre, the break-ing waves against the rocks, the UN camp with its whitewashed buildings, its heliport. Every day there are heliflights to Beirut and back again. At night, occasionally, when he hears the heli taking off he knows that a UN soldier in the mountains is either dead or seriously wounded. They are brought to the Polish Unifil hospital and if badly injured make the journey by heli to Rambam Hospital in Haifa.

He knew some soldiers who had been killed – a Ghanaian sergeant called Mike who rolled down a wadi in his water truck, a Nepalese called Kader who died during a shelling, a Fijian by the name of James who was shot by the Hezbollah, and an Irish corporal called Smithy who died as the result of a fall in Cyprus. He owed Khalil $210. Khalil crossed the sum off as goods paid for – he knew some Mingi Street men who chased for their money when a soldier died. Distasteful – some people have no mirror to their soul.

Had he?

Yes. Most times. Yes.

Except that one time. Yes?

Yes.

5

Wearily, he inches for the small bedroom upstairs. It is a compact room with a balcony affording a view of distant hills. The floor tiles are tan coloured and patterned in places with diamond shaped blue mosaics. The walls done in eggshell blue with wooden-framed paintings depicting desert scenes. This is his room. Zarifa says so. They have not shared the same bed for two years. It is because he prefers to sleep in the Street rather than in a proper house. This irritates her to the extent that she has closed her bedroom door to his face. When he moves into the house full time he can move back in with her. She forgets how stubborn he is, forgets how much he loves and needs the Street, and forgets her roots.

He showers for half an hour, letting the warm water, heated by rooftop solar panels, wash over him.

Siesta.

Khalil tugs on the cord and closes the blinds, drops his sandals from his feet and climbs on to the bed. Lies on his back and closes his eyes. Spent.

A dog barks. A tractor drags a clanging trailer. Two women pass by, cackling at some morsel of gossip. The drone of a helicopter increases in decibels as it nears the Unifil base.

Adeeba. She has his father's thinness, also his eyes and that distance in them. She was seventeen when they left Beirut. She didn't want to come with them. Preferred to stay in their home – she had met Ossie and didn't want to leave him. Young love isn't so much blind as it is short-sighted. Ossie lived on the Green Line – that damned border dividing East and West Beirut, Muslim from Christian – apartment blocks peppered with bullet holes, walls sundered from tank shells, showing the inside of a hotel as though its façade was a section removed from a doll's house. He drove across the Green Line once, during many of the truces that were false dawns in peace moves. How many lives did the war claim? Too many. Many old friends and neighbours had been killed, especially amongst those who decided to stubborn the war out in the city. Occasionally the traders Khalil dealt with, from Beirut, whom he met in Sidon, would have news of how some of his neighbours were getting on. It got so bad that in the end he told the traders not to tell him anything about Beirut – he would take it for granted that the city burned.

Adeeba wasn't a happy child. Zarifa spoiled her. Ruined her. Let her have her own way in so many small matters and yet failed to understand, when Adeeba hit her teens, why she couldn't 'control' her. If you don't vary the diet when they're small then you can't change it when they're older. He was the father figure, something for the two women to unite and rebel against. Adeeba came with them to Naqoura in a sulk – prompted by a bullet that had flown over her head and crashed into a man who had been leaving the shop. The sound, the passing breeze of the bullet, the man's screams of agony, clutching his leg, not so gentle a persuader.

Ossie followed.

Stayed a year, married Adeeba and took her back to the city. A sinecure gendarme waiting for the war to fizzle to a close so he could take up his office again. Ossie worked for a short while in the shop, pocketing dollars he didn't think Khalil knew about. Khalil never said anything about his decreasing profit margin, said only that it was time for Ossie to leave. Why create a scene? It would have only served to cause friction between husband and wife, and already there was a growing tension – catching like fire – he would not fan the flames. He was less than happy that Adeeba had chosen Ossie for a husband. He had all the personality of skin shed by a snake. He was nothing to look at – small upturned nose, eyes sunken a little under a prominent forehead.

His attitude, a breed of arrogance, relayed to Khalil the knowledge that his son-in-law would never be promoted. Arrogant men might succeed, but stupid arrogant men – never.

Zarifa fought with him when Adeeba left on that rain sodden day.

'You should have spoken with her – persuaded her to stay.'

As though he should have tried outright instead of dropping hints for her to delay her departure date – let Ossie go on ahead, get things organized. Adeeba never answered.

'It was not my place.'

'Your place? What isn't your place? You are her father.'

'I always was.'

'What do you mean?'

'I mean that you indulged her when she was young – overruled anything I said in connection to what Adeeba should and shouldn't do or be let have.'

'So what, Khalil? You've washed your hands of her?'

'No – she wouldn't listen to me when I dropped hints that she should not marry him – what am I to do? She is a woman now, not a child – I can only advise and yes, after that, after the advice, I wash my hands.'

'With a son you would have been more forceful in your opinions.'

'We'll never know that, will we, for sure?'

It wasn't so much what he said as it was the way he said it – saying things without saying them, blaming her for the fact that he never had a son.

He has a pain that Zarifa might be aware of but will never understand. The sort of pain only a man can experience when he sees other men at play with their young sons. It is a pain fraught with guilt because he loves Adeeba and in truth the love he feels for her would have measured equally with the love he would have had for a son.

Daoud – look at him, the poor unfortunate – a father who doesn't want him. Not fit to carry the name.

His thoughts quieten as sleep encroaches. Then . . .

Another man had a father.

You forgot that, Khalil, didn't you?

He sighs, opens his eyes. No.

He was married, too.

You forgot that too, didn't you? That he might have had a son.

The tongue in his head is sharp. Hurts. But he sleeps, although the sleep is unsettled and full of disturbing dreams.

He wakes late in the evening. The room is in complete darkness. He is warm and comfortable and free of pain – doesn't want to move. The shop!

Reaches for a bedside touch lamp – presses once for weak light, another for a stronger light and another he hopes for a brighter light, but the light dies and on his next touch he settles for the weak glow.

After seven. He has slept for how long? A little over six hours – the longest he has slept for months. The shop!

Ah.

He opens at six. Always. If he wasn't there to open up he ensured that someone else would, Zarifa or Joey Zhaber, his part-time assistant who died last year, Allah be good to him – an honest man.

No more always open at six, no more the time hub around which his life revolved. He supposes on the back of a deep sigh that change is inevitable. Still, he can open up at eight – it is Friday, the Street is usually busy – if he doesn't spread his net then who knows what fish might escape? It doesn't matter that his shop is no longer seen as an Aladdin's cave by the troops – a few will wander in and out and one or two might chat for a while, sit and have coffee. Even if they buy nothing they will have helped to pass the evening and it'll feel like old times again – when the Street was rich with soldiers and he was of good health, chatting and joking with them, learning about places and people he would never see. When the burning motivation was there to make another dollar, because each dollar added to his wallet he believed was a stepping stone to a better life someplace else.

Where had he wanted to go? The States. To cousins in

New Jersey – dreaming of a world without Israeli half-tracks, Hezbollah rockets, SLA extortion men, bombs and rifles and pistols and warplanes breaking the sound barrier. Away, harbouring a dream that deep down he knew he would never chase.

He dresses in blue slacks and navy short-sleeved shirt, sandals.

Zarifa is in the sitting room watching TV.

'You should have stayed in bed, Khalil, I would have brought you up some tea in about an hour.'

'I have to get to the shop.'

'It is O.K. Adeeba is there.'

'I see.'

'She took the car.'

'More dents.'

'As if you never crashed.'

'I have not – never!'

'You forget that time in Tibnin at the roundabout, when we went to visit your cousin.'

'That man crashed into me – you were there, woman, in the back, you know what happened.'

'It's still a crash – doesn't matter who was to blame – you were involved in a crash.'

Can't win with the woman. Never could. The chessboard holds only her pieces.

A kerosene heater glows on a thick Persian rug. A new

model that doesn't stink the air with a dank oily smell, unlike the one in his shop. Zarifa asks how he is feeling?

'O.K.'

'The pain?'

'Comes and goes. When it comes it stays longer and hurts more.'

'You have your pills?'

'I have my pills.'

'You would like something to eat?'

'Some cheese, olives, pitta bread – plain food is better for me.'

Zarifa stirs her feet into carpet slippers. Yawns. When she rises she is close to him.

How the years have shrunken her. Yet, she retains her old vitality. It is easy to imagine her having a long life as a widow. A healthy woman all her life – what a fortunate thing to be able to say! Long may she remain strong.

He settles in front of the TV, an itch in him to slip on his jacket and make for the Street.

Changes channels – nothing much on – the news always grim – more trouble in the mountains.

Rolls a cigarette and lights up. Zarifa brings in a tray and sets it on a green-tiled coffee table. Pours black tea into two floral-patterned glasses, chases the tea with spoonfuls of sugar and stirs, the spoon tinkling.

'You are staying the night, Khalil?'

A question or a command? Something coaxing in her tone, like a reward on offer.

'I might.'

'The shop will be safe for one night – Adeeba will take care of things.'

He shrugs.

'You can go down early in the morning.'

'I don't know – I doubt very much if I will sleep tonight.'

'Perhaps, with luck you won't.'

He nods. Shoots her a look – is she . . .?

'Drink up your tea,' she says.

She is.

6

His father's name was Izzat. And all his life he lived in the village of Al Hinniyeh, situated about 10 km from the coastal road, in a small house within walking distance of orange and lemon groves which he owned and worked.

A dirt track led from the groves to the village of Al Mansuri where he met and later wed Khalil's mother, Basma.

Khalil has only a vague memory of his mother. So vague he wonders if he conjectured the memory of her from old sepia photographs on the kitchen cabinet. A cabinet fashioned from cedar, washed almost yellow by time, parked across from the back door, so she could see who came and went.

She had hazel eyes and short dark hair, a motherly look for someone so young, and she had to be young in the photograph for she died at nineteen. An intestinal disorder, something that no doubt can be cured quite easily today, and possibly could have been back then if Izzat had got her to Tyre Hospital in time. Khalil's father lied, of course, but perhaps lies were necessary for Khalil to hear at that tender age. He had begun to ask awkward questions and the truth was too awkward for him to comprehend.

On a summer's evening, when the two of them sat on blue plastic chairs in the back garden, Izzat said she died on the way to Tyre. A cold winter's night, the stars vibrant in the heavens, a full moon washing silvery on the ocean and your mother writhing in agony in the back seat of Dr Ata's car. 'You remember Dr Ata, Khalil?'

Nodded. He did. The kind, heavily wrinkled man who was doctor to ten villages. Grey bearded with protuberant eyes he lived in a house full of books, maps and old paintings, musty walls and rank smelling carpets, dog hairs thickening their piles.

'He couldn't save her. No one could.'

'What happened?'

'She drank something.'

'What, what did she drink?'

Izzat shrugged and said he didn't know. Touched his chin and tapped his finger there.

'Didn't the doctors know – weren't tests carried out?'

'No – there was no need. No tests, no postmortem. We knew . . .'

Khalil did not know what his father meant when he said 'postmortem' and the tone, the unreadable features, didn't encourage him to ask.

At the time it seemed very strange to him that someone could die from drinking something. He was seven years old when his father began talking to him about his mother – by the time he was seventeen he knew the truth concerning the circumstances of his mother's death. The lies peeled away layer by layer according to his birthdays.

She poisoned herself.

She had not been happy for some time. Sometimes at night Izzat awakened to find her bedspace empty and he would search for her – once he found her in the fields, standing naked, staring up at the moon, her arms spread. When he called her name she didn't answer. He was afraid of her that night and also feared for her. There were bandits in the hills, jackals, wild pigs and stray dogs – all creatures with different hungers to quell – wadis with treacherous drops.

People began to talk about her – saying she was *madjnoun* – saying she had a devil inside her. Another time he found her walking the road with a basket of oranges on her head – in the pitch of night, walking roads without even knowing her own name. Quiet during the day but prone to erupt into song at the most inopportune time – at the funeral of the Imam of Haris for instance, when she had to be escorted from the mosque – the section where no woman was permitted to enter. When she lost her temper she was a she-devil – hissing and flashing her nails and throwing insults and curses.

She stabbed him once, in the shoulder. The wound required eight stitches. And maybe Khalil you don't remember this, it is for the best if you do not – she slapped you quite hard across the face, drawing blood. You were three years old. You had taken some sweets from a tray, her sweets, chocolates wrapped in shiny papers. She caught you. After that, not after the stabbing, I told her she was going away. After that she did what she did.

Now you know why the boys of the village call you the son of the *madjnoun* woman. He has a small locket and photograph of his mother that he keeps in a drawer in his shop's back room. Snapped before the *madjnoun* sickness took hold of her.

When the old man died Khalil's uncles drank arrack and smoked from his father's water pipe, speaking good things about their dead brother. How hard he worked, how generous he was, how he had done well for himself, coming to buy his own groves. A pity he married the wrong woman – if he had married another, the fat girl, can't remember her name, from Madjil Silm, he would have had a lot of sons. Men like Izzat deserved a lot of sons. They nodded. Like sages of old, oracles in a room clouded with burning incense. The water bubbled in the pipe's glass bowl, the heat rising to keep the flakes of hemp smouldering. Yes, he should have kept well away from the Al Mansuri woman.

Father's sisters chatted and haggled, complained to each other about lazy husbands. Raged, they all raged when they discovered that Izzat had sold off the orange and lemon groves for a pittance.

'Why did he sell them?' asked one of Khalil.

'I don't know.'

'You should know – didn't you speak to him? Were you not alone with him most of the time?' Another voice.

'Not about selling the groves. And yes I was alone with him most of the time – especially during the last weeks he spent dying.'

They let the barbed arrow fly over their heads without comment.

Family? They were quick to come view his corpse, the same ones who didn't visit him when he lived. Ironic.

'He sold them – and the money?'

'Money?'

'Yes?' A hard voice.

'Father was ill for a long time.'

Silence.

'There were hospital bills, doctors' fees – these had to be paid – funeral expenses.'

They said nothing.

These were coarse people, with ideas. With families of their own to fend for.

Scratching at subsisting. No honour, no dignity in being poor.

The house meant nothing to him without his father's breath and he told them they could have it. He knew by their eyes that they saw his mother in him.

A two-roomed house with a wooden veranda out front that Izzat had spent weeks making. A cousin of his has the place now. The old house knocked down and a new one built in its stead. The façade of the new house is scarred with bullet holes.

Khalil walked away. On a sunny Saturday morning he packed his mother's case and walked briskly from the house. There was no one left to tend the flowers and shrubs his mother used to care for and no one to sand and paint the wooden veranda, caress his father's name that Khalil had carved on a support beam and also the date – 14 May 1946.

Khalil was sixteen.

A world at war had not overly affected the villagers of South Lebanon. Recession meant nothing to people who had always been poor, the deprivation worsening the higher the mountain roads climbed.

Al Hinniyeh situated on the lower slopes wasn't among the poorest of the poor. But that didn't make it feel any richer.

They are all gone now, his father's people. And soon he will join them – there had also been a younger brother, two years old, who died from meningitis. Izzat mentioned him once on a winter's day as they worked in the groves, filling baskets with ripe oranges for the markets in Tyre and Sidon.

There are times he thinks of his father's wizened face, his grey stubble and sunken lips caused by absent teeth, the striped garment he wore, the fez minus its tassel, and he sees how hard it was for him to stand and watch the woman he loved slowly go mad.

He never remarried, although he often visited a woman in Qana, a widow with many sons, who lived in a corner house near the village square. An obese woman, Khalil had heard.

This was something his father didn't tell him – he was at an age when he had started to learn things for himself. To defend his mother, to try and recoup some dignity for her, he told his friends and anyone who would listen that losing his brother drove his mother mad.

He was sure it made them think of her in a new light. That there had been a reason behind her insanity. They would look at him and nod, continue plucking mint leaves or sucking on their pipes or cigarettes, saying nothing until someone moved the conversation on.

In the end he gave up talking about her. No one wanted to know. Old bones in the grave was not fresh news, his aunt said.

Izzat said that when Khalil's brother died he carried his son's dead body on the back of his donkey and buried him in a grave near an olive tree on a foothill. It had taken him a day to shovel beyond earth, rock and root, the sweat thick on his brow and spine as he prayed to Allah for his son's soul.

'Why Papa, bury him there, on his own?'

'To stop your mother going to the cemetery and taking him home – he was three weeks dead and she would not let me take him. She hid him from me. I could get no good out of her – then I walked in on top of her one day, unexpectedly, and I took him from her.'

'Where was I?'

'You lived with my brother in Tibnin.'

'My brother's name?'

'Yusef.'

'Where is—'

'I forget. It was such a long time ago.'

'He was left there, Papa, no – why didn't you put him with Mother in her grave?'

'I could not find his grave.'

Izzat's face turned hard, his eyes dimmed. As though he looked inwards at the lie he had told.

The truth?

Revealed hours before Izzat died, that jackals had disturbed Yusef's grave and there was nothing left except strips of his clothing.

Khalil imagined Izzat in the dark of night, a beam of torchlight running along the ground as he dug, hoping he was wrong, that the old mound of red soil, the disturbed rocks he had marked the grave with, was not what he suspected – a jackal's scratchings.

The cry of a father doing something he would not have seen himself do in his worst nightmare – a cry that would have rent the night air and unsettled the hearts of those who heard.

His father loved the wilds. Often they would set out for three or four days with his grey donkey and walk the hills and mountains, the wadis, sleeping at night by a wood fire, eating some *khoubiz*, unleavened bread, and *makanek*, lamb sausages.

This was a time before the civil war. A time between wars.

Izzat often pointed towards Palestine and showed him the corridors used by smugglers – centuries old these trails, routes of commerce and of flight. The hills and wadis scored with caves too numerous to record – a man could hide in them for life, if he had enough food and water, if he wanted to be a hermit.

Palestine. Izzat never referred to it as Israel. Israel didn't exist. When it came into being, when the news crackled in the kitchen on the walnut Philips radio he bought in Tyre, his eyes moistened and his lower lip trembled. Light failing he faced south and stared long and hard at the occupied land.

Khalil and Izzat while working in the groves had watched the Palestinian refugees stream along the coastal road, making for the village of Ar Rashidiyah, next to the sea, south of Tyre.

A procession of colours, of walking wounded, of crushed spirits, of dejected faces – young and old, a long river of misery.

And still they live in the village, a village surrounded by a swell of tin shacks and roughly constructed concrete dwellings, a growing swell. If they walk to the water's edge, let the sea lap at their toes and bend their torso forward they can see Palestine – a chalk coloured promontory with sea caves, where the Israelis have their border with Lebanon. They hold title deeds of lands that belonged to their fathers, worthless in the eyes of a conquering race.

The sun goes down on their anger, night after night, month after month, year after year.

His father used to say that the Palestinians should never have left their homeland. All should have stayed – time would have won their war for them.

He had a pair of flintlock pistols with brass butts. Varnished, maintained in near pristine condition, that he sold to buy a .303 rifle and some ammunition. He bought the rifle in the souk in Baghdad, had been told that Lawrence of Arabia had used its butt to kill a Turkish soldier.

'There might be a war, son – we will need some protection.'

'Fight the Israelis, Papa?'

'No. The Palestinians.'

Khalil looked up from the book he had opened. The light dim where his father sat. He could not distinguish his features.

'Son, if you bring someone in to live with you they will take over the house within months, you will find yourself cooking what they want to eat, listening to the radio programmes they want to listen to – they take over. It happens.'

And while his father never got to fire his rifle it happened as he said it would, many years after his death.

Khalil had the weight of his father's money in his leather pouch; dollars Izzat kept from the sale of the groves, willing it to his son, making him promise not to part with any of it. You can read and write and add and subtract – shake the dust of this place out of your clothes, be the *madjnoun* woman's son no more. Go.

7

After their lovemaking he lies awake in the softness of the night. No wind, no traffic noise, the sound of the sea absent. Neither the droning of Israeli warplanes, nor the thudding of illumination flares, nor shell nor gunfire interrupts the slow beating of his heart in his ear. The land sleeps quietly – a silence unmarred. Like a night plucked from his childhood. Closes his eyes. He is a child again.

Through a hole in a sheet draped across wire to screen his bed he watched his father sitting in the kitchen, sipping at coffee, reading his newspaper that he had spread on the table, turning his prayer beads, the boy praying too, for his father never to go *madjnoun*.

His father had grown sparse of hair and physique, as if the mountain winds had hewn him to certain specifications. The flesh taut about his high cheekbones, leather skin cracked like fissures in sun-baked earth. His gums bright red and no longer the solid foundations that they had been for his fine sturdy teeth. In his eyes a dimming light. Khalil wanted to slip out from behind the screen and stand before him, touch his cheeks where his tears trailed, but he didn't, because that would have embarrassed Papa – made light of his daily effort to be strong, to show strength. And yet there was something strong about him, pliable bone. His tears fell quietly. A soul cleansing itself.

The black of night, the cold in the house, the rising wind caressing the depths of the wadis, the Philips radio on low, the creaks of bed springs as his father's body settled in the mattress – his sole luxury – an expensive bed, previously owned by Dr Ata who died in it the previous winter, sold by his nephew who burned all his books and maps and carpets. Clouding the skies with smoke and black floating crisps of another's earthly treasures – debris of a past.

Zarifa sleeps. He had forgotten how good it was, the mingling of two bodies, the way she nibbled on his ear – how the years were driven away for those few precious minutes. They were teenagers again – in Beirut, the love capital of the world – the Paris of the Middle East.

In those days Khalil worked in a biscuit factory by day and went to college three evenings a week, studying appliance repair. Later he quit the biscuit job to take up an opening in an electrical shop he was afterwards to buy out with his savings and his father's money. Keeping on the staff, including the very pretty secretary, Zarifa, whom he had met briefly in the Bekaa Valley two summers ago. She thought him shy and awkward, fearful of women. At times she wondered if he were, you know?

She said this over tea in the office. He almost choked on his spicy falafel. She had knocked and entered his office, carrying a tea tray. Usually she did this and they would exchange pleasantries and then she would leave. On this occasion he noticed firstly that there were two cups, secondly that she had closed the door behind her and thirdly that she was primed to say something in a hurry before she changed her mind, or the opportunity to speak was lost to her.

'Mister Abbas—'

'Please, it's Khalil, it's always been Khalil, why the change?'

A pay rise? Hardly. He paid a little over the going rate to all his staff.

She let out a stream of words that left her breathless and struck him dumb.

'Well?' she said, finally.

'You, you . . .'

Her hand went up in a traffic gendarme's stop signal, 'It is true – I have seen you looking at me many times. And when I look back you look away.'

To deny was to lie. He shrugged and said he liked her and was attracted to her in a physical way, too. But his experiences of women were not good ones. And no, no, he was not homosexual. The very idea!

'I felt that if I didn't talk to you first you would never talk to me. I mean really talk.'

'That may be so.'

'Do you want me to stay?'

He got up and walked to the office window, looked out at Beirut's rush hour traffic chaos. Most of the staff had left for lunch, except for old Henri the mute Moroccan who lived in a small room above the shop. When they knocked on the door Zarifa told the friends she usually lunched with to go on ahead.

They talked at length and laughed a lot. He didn't tell her about his mother. He never spoke of her, other than to say she was dead. He would often speak of his father and his hard life, without explaining why it was hard.

Zarifa piece by piece, week by week, chipped away at his wall of fear and suspicion and in the end he submitted gratefully and without regret – never a single regret. Bared his soul to her with the exception of two things – never a word about the *madjnoun* woman. Never. And never a word about the night he stood by and watched and allowed an evil act to take place.

He is one of love's lucky men – Zarifa doesn't probe the

way some women do when they sense that their men
harbour secrets, as a consequence he has not lied to her. She
is a friend who doesn't question the reason behind a favour
being asked of her. Khalil contemplates a cigarette but Zarifa
would boil. Bladder aches but he doesn't want to leave
Zarifa's side – there is a strength she gives him or he draws
from her. He is not sure. Perhaps a giving and a taking. The
sum of their marriage. Yet he has been sleeping away from
her – what sort of a complex creature is he?

Adeeba had called around midnight, to say she had locked
the shop and was staying the night as planned. How did he
sleep on such an old and lumpy mattress? She had bought a
new one and fresh sheets and a duvet from the Top Shop.
They had nice jeans too, real Levis, but there were holes in
the pockets and some had no pocket liners at all – genuine
Mingis.

Business?

She had some Fijians in. Touched much, bought nothing.
A Ghanaian paid $10 off his account. A Nepalese soldier
bought a cheap watch and a talking alarm clock, you know
the one with the American accent? 'Seven-thirty a.m. – time
to get up.' It took him a long time to choose between that
and a clock that crowed. 'Oh, and an Irishman called in to
speak with you.'

'His name?' He already knew – confirmed by a touch of
ice in his spine.

'He didn't say. I told him to call back tomorrow.'

'Irish?' Be sure. Doubt breeds Hope.

'Yes, I'm sure, I thought at first he might have been Polish – he had this stiff, formal manner that some of them have.'

'I see.'

'He said he was an MP.'

'From the hills or the HQ?'

'Father – such questions!'

He sighed. He liked to be in control of his shop, to know everything that went on. It was like a captain seeing an ex-command of his break waves without him. The ship didn't appear to cut through the waters quite right. O'Driscoll? Yes. Who else, but the living ghost?

Zarifa's snores are soft. She sleeps on her side with her back to him. She has presented him with a difficult choice. In truth there should be no choice, he should do as she wishes – move into the house, use its comfort, enjoy her pleasures. But he was never a quitter. The shop occupies his mind. If he stays at home Zarifa will remind him of his illness. He will not be allowed to forget that this year there is no winter for him.

Still, shouldn't he spend his last days with his wife? In one sense isn't he lucky to know that death is going to call for him, instead of making an unscheduled visit?

There are many souls to whom the opportunity of tidying their affairs and saying goodbye to loved ones was denied –

they would have swapped choice of deaths with him, gladly.

But perhaps he has been spared a quick death for a purpose. Perhaps his soul has been presented with an opportunity to make amends? After he dies there will be no one left to do the right thing, if it is the right thing.

He allows a short time to elapse before deciding to rise. He touches Zarifa's hair, her naked shoulder, and eases from bed. Drifts into the bathroom to leak and then shower. He dresses in a white T-shirt, clean underwear (new, from Israel, expensive but better quality than that available in Mingi Street) and blue tracksuit pants. Pads about the kitchen in his bare feet making sticking noises on the tiles, delaying sipping at his coffee just to enjoy the anticipation and for his senses to linger on the rich thick fragrance.

Lights his first cigarette of the new day. Takes the coffee out back to watch the sun climbing high and quickly to its position.

Beautiful morning.

A morning for the living.

Perhaps O'Driscoll hadn't called into the shop – it could well be a different MP. Or a former customer who had returned to Lebanon. Perhaps his photograph is in the albums Khalil keeps in the shop. Photographs of the soldiers he had befriended and invited to meals on special occasions. More than likely it is over some trivial matter – sometimes Khalil has information for the MPs – knowledge he parts with because he owes the MPs favours for chasing down his credit defaulters.

About who was breaking into Unifil stores. Which soldiers to watch out for, the days and times they made their runs to Beirut, who on the Street is supplying them with the goods, the going rate for a drop.

There were people on the Street who wore their greed on their sleeves. Like Kasni, his distant cousin, who collected money from the Mingi Street traders and called it tax instead of extortion. He is a man who in a temper speaks with bullets instead of hard words. There is no compromise with him, just an end.

Confused.

Live here or in the house?

Compromise?

Hmm.

Khalil drowns his pills with water. The pain has stirred, woken from its slumber. Only Allah knows when his next respite will be.

Voice. Listen, Khalil. O'Driscoll *called*. As a Christian might say, not the Trinity, not quite your Father, Son and Holy Spirit, but two out of three, eh? For sure.

Zarifa joins him at the table. She wears a light blue kaftan with an embroidered gold neckline. Her hair brushed and damp from the shower.

'More coffee, Khalil?'

'La – two cups already, it is enough.'

'I'll pour you a cup to look at.'

He smiles.

'How are you this morning?' she says.

'Fine, and you?'

She blushes.

Ah, still the tints of youth.

'I meant your health – your pain,' she says, waving at a fly.

'And that's what I meant, too, your health.'

'My health is fine, thank you.'

Buttering some toast she looks under his eyebrows at him. She has aged well.

Like him she is a liberal Muslim. Like him she prays, but unlike him she has a pure belief in the hereafter.

'The shop,' she says, finally.

'Yes?'

'Adeeba can manage it, I think.'

Before he has time to speak she continues.

'Why don't you work in shifts? Let Adeeba work the evenings and you the mornings?'

'Is it safe for her to stay there at night?'

'It is – you know it is. And she has only to knock on the door for Dahab. And you have a shop full of mobile phones.'

'Evenings are when it is busy.'

'Adeeba—'

'Does not know to whom she can give credit.'

'You could teach her, and besides . . .'

He sighs, massages his side. Her words had trailed away, her lips moving for moments after she cut them off.

'Say it.'

'Nothing.'

'Go on.'

'No. It is not right for me to say it.'

'It was to think it, though.'

'Very well, if you must know, I was thinking that you should not be giving credit.'

She's right. How could he have let that fact slip by him? When he dies the money he is owed will be forgotten about by many, slates wiped clean. Zarifa and Adeeba will not chase the soldiers for money. In many instances, sure, they will pay up, for most are honourable, but the few who won't are a few too many. Although business isn't great Kasni still expects his weekly cut. His insistence has as much to do with the closure of some Mingi shops as has the declining troop numbers.

'Yes, it is probably right that I stop giving credit. After all, the shop will be closed when I am gone. Isn't that so?'

Zarifa nods, 'It will.'

'It has served us well, Zarifa.'

'Yes, it has.'

'Perhaps I will close it next month – tidy my affairs.'

Zarifa sits upright, 'We can take a holiday, after the wedding.'

The wedding? Kasni's sister, Najia – yes, he had forgotten. 'Where?'

'Beirut.'

'Perhaps, yes – but here, home here is holiday enough for me.'

He let her think on that for a few moments before adding, 'And I think I will work every second evening in the shop.'

Zarifa frowns.

Compromise.

'Every second evening you stay here?'

'Yes, with you, here.'

'Until?'

'Until I close the shop – then, then – till whenever.'

Zarifa agrees.

8

Khalil waits in the sitting room for Adeeba to appear. It is after midday and she had been due home at eleven. When he dialled her mobile she said he was to give her five minutes. 'I am in my car – on the way.'

Did she say that? Really? 'My car.'

I'm not dead yet, Adeeba, he thinks, feeling as grim as a grey day. Slip of the tongue – of course – just being paranoid.

He rings again but gets no reply. Has something happened to her? Ossie? No. He won't show his face, not yet, until Khalil is gone, then he might decide to visit, just to see what he can bully from two women.

He considers walking to the village but the sun shimmers on the road in lazy waves and he doesn't trust his legs to carry him that far. Besides he is in a half temper with a tongue primed to wound. Best he stays put and works on remaining calm.

Khalil hates waiting about.

Zarifa says, coming in from the line with clothes, that he should take the whole day off – read a book, watch TV, there's a good video in the cupboard called *Braveheart* – she bought it in Elsa's, the quality is all right, except for the first couple of minutes when it rolls a little. He hasn't the patience to watch, anxious to be at the shop.

The old familiar sound of his Merc growls its arrival out front. Door slams.

Women have no respect for cars. How many times has he told Adeeba that there is no need to slam a car door? Zarifa is the same, only she slams plugs into sockets – one day, he tells her, the socket will kick back.

'Good morning, Father,' Adeeba says, entering on a false breeze of energy.

She looks tired. Hands him the keys.

'I put a sign on the shop saying "Back shortly," O.K.?'

'These are the keys of *my* car, Adeeba?'

Perplexed she says, 'Yes, why?'

'Ah, it is nothing, never mind.'

'I'm sorry about the delay but I got talking to Dahab and oh she's so frustrating – she wanted to know what the hell I was playing at – telling her boy there was no work for him.'

'Daoud?'

'Yes. That's him.'

'He works for me.'

'Oh, you don't need him now that I'm here.'

'He works for me, Adeeba.'

'I did tell them I would speak with you.'

'Yes, and you have and now you know – I like to have the boy around me. He doesn't have an easy life. I make it a little easier for him. O.K., Adeeba?'

Raises her eyebrows to show she means no offence and to signal her puzzlement at the strength of his argument.

'There's fifty dollars in the drawer – it took me an age to open – very stiff – and seven single bills in your old biscuit tin.'

He nods.

'Not brisk business, Father.'

'No.'

'What used to be your daily takings?'

'Best ever was eight hundred dollars but usually three to four hundred dollars a day.'

'Your worst?'

'Eight dollars – usually it's twenty to thirty dollars a day. Except for the weekends when the troops come in to pay off their bills. Then it's higher.'

'How much credit have you given?'

Sharp Adeeba. Good. Good to see that she's thinking business and not about that wastrel of a husband.

'I have about five thousand dollars' worth of stock out.'

Adeeba. He used to worry about the *madjnoun* coming out in her. While slightly nervous and flighty, Adeeba is fine, thank Allah. His prayers have been answered while Adeeba's have not – but she has no child to lose, therefore the risk of suffering her grandmother's fate has been minimized. Adeeba, Adeeba, what will become of you when I am gone?

He slips into his sandals and says goodbye to Zarifa and Adeeba in the kitchen.

'You'll be here for dinner?' Zarifa queries.

'Em, maybe today I'll walk the street, see how things are going with the others – catch up on the local gossip. So, I'll get something to eat maybe in the Ramada – a pepper steak.'

He tries to ignore the look of hurt on Zarifa's face, but can't. She wounds easily but only at certain times and for seemingly no reason.

'Would you like to join me – say at two – when it is less busy – you too, Adeeba?'

'I won't,' Zarifa says.

'I'm going to the Twilight for a swim and maybe take a pizza in the hotel restaurant later,' Adeeba says.

Zarifa has gone a little too grand for the Street. She prefers her feet to walk in Tyre, Sidon and Beirut. She says that Mingi Street is a harbour for pirates and drug dealers. Devils the lot of them. Cutting at him, too, trying to make him see that she has another reason for wanting him out of there. She has come up in the world, as he has, but he prefers to live and work amongst the dross.

A tug of war for him – the Street on one side and Zarifa on the other.

She does not understand that if has to die he would rather die in the old shack from where the two of them rebuilt their world and not where they ended up.

He drives slowly and parks outside Dahab's. Out of the car he sees where Adeeba hosed down the concrete under his shop's black and white awning and the Perspex windows. Dahab's – the plastic seats under the Budweiser sun canopy are empty, the pages of a comic on the round table held in place by pebbles. The breeze riffles the dog-eared corners as though eager to read on.

Khalil shows his head in Dahab's.

Daoud sits on a tattered sofa taking in TV while Dahab sorts clothes into piles for washing. Noticing Khalil she smiles and brings his eyes to Daoud before raising her own to the corrugated ceiling. A cat then another start to meow under the sofa.

The smell of cat piss is pungent. A gas fire sits idle in the corner, its brown aluminium skin dented and scraped, leaning in at a corner where its wheel is missing.

Two bedrooms leading from the main room are screened with curtains, redolent of another house in another time.

'Daoud, are you ready for some work?'

Without looking at him, the child says, 'Adeeba told me to go away and stay away.'

'Ah, you work for me not Adeeba.'

The boy sighs, 'I have another job, now.'

Khalil buries a smile, 'Oh, I see. But I need you to work for me – we have a deal, your watch, remember?'

Silence.

'Tell you what – to make up for the confusion I will give you the watch as a bonus, and you can start earning your money from today – eh?'

Daoud sits up, looks down as his bare feet, 'I suppose – I haven't signed any contract with my new boss, yet—'

'Good! That's settled, come on—'

'Will you give me a contract?'

Seven years old – contract! The power of TV, no doubt.

'Sure, we can make out one now – tell me what you want – we have to deal, remember.'

Daoud disappears behind a curtain. Rustling noises, a scraping noise – drawing something from under his bed.

Dahab, he notices, only now – what is becoming of his perception? In decline like the rest of him, he supposes.

'Your cheek, what happened to your cheek?'

'Nothing.'

He advances, squinting. One side of her face is bright red, as though she has been exposed to the sun – strawberry mark on olive flesh!

'Nothing, Dahab?'

'Khalil, don't concern yourself.'

'I would not be a neighbour if I did not show some concern.'

Silence. Broken by Daoud's, 'Got it!'

'Aziz?' Khalil breathes.

Daoud emerges, 'Here, Khalil, I have paper and a pencil.'

Slowly, Khalil pulls his eyes away from Dahab, wondering what on earth the small boy beside him had witnessed or listened to last night. Adeeba, had she not heard?

'Ink, Daoud, we'll use my pen – you can erase pencil lead, erase your contract. Now that's not the way of businessmen like us – let's go next door and come to an arrangement.'

The boy wears blue shorts, loose red and white T-shirt and old flip-flops. He carries the dust and perspiration of days on his thin olive arms and legs. His short black hair is matted and his eyes reveal a certain angst.

Inside the shop he leaves the 'Closed' sign in place, indicates Daoud to a chair as he sits behind his desk. Tugs on the stiff drawer and after checking that the hour is right hands the G Shock to the boy – can he tell the time?

Daoud rests his wrist on his thigh to buckle the straps around it. The watch falls down the back of his hand but this doesn't appear to bother him.

'I can see the time in the dark if I just press this – my friend has one – he wears it just like me.'

'What time is it now?'

'It is after one.'

'Good man, one o'clock, Daoud.'

He writes up a few lines on lined paper, then turns it around and asks Daoud to read and if satisfied to sign his name at the bottom.

The boy can't read. Makes a bad fist at pretending that he can.

Khalil says, the thought just lighting on him, 'Why aren't you at school?'

'I don't like school – I stay home and help my mother – we sort out the clothes. And I am there if my father comes.'

'Did he visit last night?'

'Uh-huh.'

'You know if you are going to be a businessman you must go to school.'

'Why – I can count – count up to a hundred.'

'Do you have a certificate from the school to say this?'

'No . . .'

Scratches at the floor with the tips of his flip-flops.

'Think about going back to school – if you want to be my partner then I'll need to see that you're going to school.'

'O.K. – I'll ask my mother if I can go back.'

Khalil realizes that Aziz is refusing to fund the boy's education. He will have a talk with Aziz, surely there must be a way of getting through to the man. He has a new wife, a new house and a new car – a few dollars towards his son's future should not be too much to give.

He has buried one son.

Why mark this boy?

But first Dahab, he must speak with her.

He tells Daoud to count his stock on the shelves and not to open up until his return.

Dahab's hand keeps going to her chin.

'No, Khalil – you must not ask Aziz for money.'

'Why not? It is his duty.'

'If you ask him he will think that I am the tongue behind the question – no – you don't understand.'

'I understand only too well, Dahab.'

She stands the iron upright and looks at him. He is close enough to smell the ointment on her cheek and the smell of a pressed shirt.

'He ironed my face last night.'

'I thought so.'

'I screamed.'

'Did Daoud see?'

'I think so. He watches Aziz like a hawk, praying with his eyes that his temper lies cold.'

'What happened?'

'He wants me. I tell him to go to his new wife. He says he will afterwards. I don't usually deny him. I just go quietly with him to my room and then he stays quiet – but last night I was so tired, so tired – all day iron, all day wash – no time to visit the cemetery – you know what day it was yesterday, Khalil?'

Khalil nods. He knows now.

'My son's anniversary. Two years he is dead – and do you think Aziz knew?'

'No.'

'Or cared – do you think he cared?'

'Is there no place you can go?'

'I have a sister in Cyprus, but I wouldn't live there. And a brother in Canada – too far away – I don't think I could live—'

'You're not living here.'

'So, I should just move away?'

'Yes – if not for your own sake then for Daoud's.'

'Who will wash your clothes?'

Such a pretty smile.

'Ah, I will manage.'

'Perhaps you are right. Perhaps I should leave.'

'If it's money I can help with a little.'

'Why are you being so kind to me?'

'For Daoud's sake, Basma.'

She says, 'Basma?'

Can't undo the past. Why had his mother's name slipped out? How? He hadn't been thinking of her. A sign that she needs prayers?

Something else.

Can't stop a man swinging by his neck from an olive tree, the rope creaking, his hands bound behind his back, his eyes popping. Done in the wash of a full moon – a handful standing back, a couple of punches and kicks on the swaying body to ascertain death, to vent anger, as though murdering him hadn't vented the anger enough.

Not one death but two.

But one he is concerned with, because he wasn't there for the first – had arrived late.

He should speak with Adfal, but can't bring himself to dial his number – not yet.

9

Slowly, as he walks the street, anger consumes him. He tries but fails to recall the last time he has been this riled. This is a day of conspiracies. Adeeba delaying him to the point of sheer frustration saw him tie his tongue in knots to stop himself from verbally assaulting her. And now Aziz's actions have his veins itching to spill his blood. To take him and iron his throat from the inside out.

In addition he has hunger pangs that he suspects are false, a mirage, but which he will answer. Even if he keeps down only a little food it will be better than nothing.

It is a muggy morning, no sun and dead air. He enters The Beer Palace, run by Jesso, a raven-haired young man who recently married a woman from Al Yatun village. Khalil had been in Beirut Hospital undergoing tests and missed the ceremony and reception. Khalil used to know his father, a quiet inoffensive man who drowned after his fishing boat collided with the Black Rocks on a stormy night. He has known Jesso since he was a boy of Daoud's age.

Jesso sits behind a desk to the left of the door. Wears no shirt, just a long gold chain with a crucifix. He has a thick carpet of hair on his chest and a loose and ready smile plays on his round olive face. A cigarette burns on a glass ashtray by his hand – his fingers drip with gold rings.

He sells beer, spirits and cigarettes to the soldiers and to the messes in Unifil HQ and the Area of Operations. Khalil has heard he might be involved in smuggling to Beirut, but you hear such things in the Street, usually they are words wasted on the wind by jealous rivals. Jesso also sells food and soft drinks – the smell in his shop is a commingling of fragrant spices, cigarette smoke and strong liquor.

'Khalil, welcome, sit, sit.'

Jesso is on his feet, rounding the side of his desk, extending his hand, pulling a chair hidden from view by mid floor boxes and crates of beer and soft drinks.

'Khalil – it is good to see you.'

Khalil sits, waves a hand to calm the enthusiastic reception, but Jesso is like this with people. He is popular with the soldiers for he is never over eager to take their money – if they want they buy, if they don't that is O.K. Sit down, take a juice or a beer from the fridge. Talk. He is also fair, never uses sleight of hand with them. Khalil has heard it said that when the recent Polish rotation to Warsaw took place the Polish Customs came down particularly hard on the troops, confiscating much contraband. As a result the remaining soldiers who were due to rotate the following week asked the traders to take back their goods. They did, but only Jesso gave them the money they paid so that they suffered no loss, the others made a killing. Some of them would lick away a mound of camel dung to get at a dollar.

Jesso used to serve with the SLA Special Forces, spending many operational nights in wadi caves to fight the Amal and Palestinian guerrillas. He is a man appreciative of life – a man who stared into the mouth of a rifle, heard a click and nothing else. Misfire. Khalil knows the story. He heard it from Jesso's brother, Feek, how an Amal guerrilla in the heavy rains stole up on Jesso's three man patrol, aimed his AK-47 rifle at Jesso's face and squeezed the trigger. Click. An empty click. Hollow.

A misfire, Feek said, probably caused by excessive carbon on the firing pin or the pin itself had broken. Either way the round never left the barrel. Jesso's did.

'So, Khalil, what can I do for you? You wish to change some dollars into shekels – visit Israel, a brothel in Nahariya perhaps?'

Khalil smiles.

'No thank you, Jesso, this is just a visit. I have not called here for a long time.'

'I heard you were ill.'

'I am.'

Jesso touches under his left breast, '*Assif*, Khalil.'

Khalil closes and opens his eyes in an act of accepting the other's spoken regret.

Jesso untabs and hands Khalil a can of peach juice with Hebrew markings – in Beirut this offering and acceptance of such would see them lynched. Lynched – lynch mob – when does a person become part of one – can one be regarded as being a member even if on the mob's periphery? Yes. Yes, unless he is dumb and immobilized, yes.

'I know you like this – but something stronger, maybe?'

'La – it is too early in the day. This fine nectar is perfect, thanks.'

'You Muslims. Between non-drinkers and secret drinkers I would have a poor livelihood.'

'You Christians – you drink too much, your God will smell you coming to his altar.'

Smiles. Khalil expresses his congratulations on Jesso's marriage and Jesso his thanks for Khalil's gift, a gift of dollars – he had been honoured to receive the envelope on the day. Dahab had presented it on Khalil's behalf.

'Flee money,' Khalil says.

Jesso nods his understanding, pops the cap off a Maccabi beer and puts the neck to his mouth.

They talk some, mostly about the street traders who have

closed down and moved on, the way their shops stand like buildings in a Wild West ghost town – the way there will come a time when the whole Street will be reduced to perhaps an eighth of its current length, with just a few concrete shops remaining, erected by those who'll put their faith in the new regime – because, they both agree, the day will come when the SLA won't exist and the Israelis will sit behind their border, watching, waiting, to see the Hezbollah's next move. And people like Jesso will be out foreign. Refugees again, if wealthier this time around, cushioned by their savings, their 'flee' dollars.

'Tommy the Coffee Man trades outside Sidon, now, near the hospital – parks his van outside its walls. Convenient for him as his wife is recovering in a ward, you remember her, the way she used to beat him?' Jesso says.

'Poor Tommy – he made good coffee, almond flavoured – he had me addicted.'

'When we were kids Feek and me would sit behind his van and drink his coffee. He always looked old to us. He used to give us free coffee if we went about handing out leaflets that told people his coffee tasted great.'

'Must be eighty years old, at least.'

'If not more. His she-devil is about seventy – looks younger.'

'Good man. A good man doesn't always get a good woman.'

They talk some more, about Porno Joe and his efforts to reopen the brothel. Rose Najm and Samia Haqqi, co-owners of Mingi Street Hotel opposite Le Moulin Rouge, the deserted former brothel, objecting loudest.

Jesso rakes his fingers through his hair, a slow smile pushing up a corner of his mouth. 'Didn't they pull a Polish soldier from a watery end? After curfew Mingi Street was denied to him by the French Guard so he took to the sea, intending to swim past the hotel and on to the shore, thirty metres from his Promised Land – the women disturbed by his crazy cries for help. Had they not succeeded in throwing him a rope he would have been taken out to sea. You know, Khalil, how dangerous the currents are out around there, the rocks.'

Khalil nods. He knows – the Black Rocks should be called the Blood Rocks, 'Crazy – crazy man.'

Jesso grins, 'What's really crazy is the fact that had he completed the swim, eh – imagine him – dripping wet, knocking on the door, the place in darkness because the SLA had closed the brothel that morning.'

Khalil's eyes begin to water with mirth, 'And what happened to him?'

'Rose phoned the French Guard and they put him in the Brig.'

Continuing Jesso says that Unifil's electrical cable stores south of the old brothel had been robbed the weekend before his wedding. Coincidentally, the same weekend Rose and Samia were having their hotel extension wired. 'So, the MPs arrive to investigate the break-in and while checking the stores find a hole in the south wall. O.K.? The thieves fed the cable through this hole and on to a truck, yeah. Anyway, the MPs checking outside the stores come across Rose's cabling and thinking the thieves left it behind confiscate the lot, and don't listen to Rose and Samia. You can imagine Samia, oh, blade tongue, but it did no good. Rose rings me and I ring Sergeant O'Driscoll – Jimmy, yes, MP Coy. He often comes to my shop for a beer, to talk – he gets the cable back and Rose and Samia put on a great wedding reception. The best, believe me.'

Jesso gives a thumbs up.

'Jimmy was there, too. Hey, I've got a video of the wedding – you have time to watch?'

Khalil gives a slight wave of his hand and declines the offer for another time, when he has matters that are less pressing.

'Do you know O'Driscoll?' Jesso says.

'O'Driscoll,' Khalil murmurs, recalling the taciturn Irishman with the hard eyes. His stomach beginning to churn.

'Khalil, he called here looking for information about some old murders that happened a long time ago. A Yank and an Irish guy were hanged – you know of it?'

Khalil rubs his chin with his palm, 'A little.'

'How long ago – twenty years?'

'No – not that far back.'

'Ah, you might be able to help him.'

'Help, in what way, help?'

'The body – to help find his father's body.'

Khalil nods, 'It's a long time ago – many have lost their lives since then. A lot of bodies were never found, will never be found.'

He hopes Jesso doesn't detect the slight tremor in his tone, and that his stress doesn't reveal itself in his pallor.

Jesso strikes up his lighter, lifts the dead cigarette from the ashtray and stokes it alive. Says through a smoke cloud, 'Well, Khalil, I remember when my father died, Jesus mind him, all we prayed for was that the sea would give him up, that we'd get him home.'

Khalil feels himself burning a little inside. His mother with Yusef – how she wouldn't let go, how he was lost to the jackals – their jubilant cries carried by the wind. Yes, it is hard to let go, even if you have the remains of a loved one it is difficult to let go.

'O'Driscoll, he . . .' Khalil trails off.

Khalil gives a series of slight nods for Jesso to go on. Allah keep the rising panic in me from overflowing.

'He is determined to find out what happened that day.'

Jesso sits behind his desk, props his elbows on its

scratched surface, fingers locking, the cigarette a stubby little turret gun. His hazel eyes wide and probing, as if he is viewing Khalil for the first time and is cautious in how he should deal with him.

'You don't look well, Khalil.'

Khalil is aware that Jesso might have heard stories. Had his father ever spoken? He was there, too – that night – he carried the rope, fashioned the nooses – Isaac Mouri did that. Jesso's smile would wither if he heard this. That is not to say he would believe. No. He would fluster and accuse Khalil of lying.

Deep down knowing he had been told the truth.

There are many men who after the night in question bowed their head in shame, refusing to discuss their involvement to the extent they denied being present at all. Done to avoid revenge, to avoid the curses of the victim's relatives falling on their family name, but mostly they denied it in order to live with themselves.

All these men now have another thing in common – they are dead, and have no questions to answer. At least not to the living.

Some died of disease, others were killed in firefights amongst themselves and against the Israelis, a couple more in bomb blasts, a few of old age – the youngest of them who should have carried the secret for far longer than Khalil are all gone.

Who did they tell?

Wives?

Sons?

Daughters?

Girlfriends?

Promises made in the sweat of the evil night – that not another soul was to know. Not a name who was present there to be breathed to other ears. Ever.

But someone might have spoken in his sleep, cried out?

Possible. Isn't he himself guilty of that from time to time?

Someone might have been there whom the mob had forgotten about or hadn't seen – a child, a shepherd, someone who had stayed at the back and slipped away, biting his hand to keep himself from vomiting?

No. That is possible, but highly unlikely.

If someone spoke then the secret has only travelled short distances and has stayed in small rooms. Has Jesso heard of such rumours?

'I am ill, Jesso.'

'Khalil, I know that O'Driscoll has called to your shop and here and other shops in Mingi.'

'I will speak with him, tell him what little I know.'

'Yes, he is a good man, I am sure. He just wants his father's body to bury, that's all.'

'That's all?'

'I mean I don't think he wants justice.'

'Justice, Jesso, here? What sort of justice would he expect? Does he not realize the impossibility of his task? Do you think there are people who can tell him what became of his father's body?'

Jesso purses his lips.

'Do you, Jesso?'

'I think he has come to recover his father's bones, that's all. I think he should get all the help that we can give.'

'We? How can you or I help him?'

'I already have, Khalil.'

Something bitter sours in Khalil's throat.

'You have – in what way?'

'I found newspaper cuttings in my father's things – cuttings about the murders, and photographs taken by journalists of a corpse swinging from a tree, the rope beside it missing its noose – it was on the ground, lying like a snake. Uncoiled.'

Khalil nods, 'I remember seeing these.'

'The corpse swinging was that of an American officer. The other, well that's the question, isn't it, Khalil, what became of the body? Of O'Driscoll's father?'

'It is. The question.'

Jesso tamps his cigarette in the ashtray, 'Do you know what I think, Khalil?'

'No. Enlighten me.'

'I think they took pity on him.'

'Is that a logical conclusion?'

'Logical conclusion, yes. Khalil, there's the Irish question – perhaps people feared that the Irish Government might have withdrawn its battalion from Lebanon if it saw one of its peacekeepers killed in such an ugly fashion.'

Jesso pauses for Khalil's response but when there is none forthcoming he shrugs, 'I don't think I'll ever be accused of being the Lebanese Sherlock Holmes.'

Khalil sips at some of his peach juice and leans over to place the almost full soft drink into the bin beside Jesso's desk.

He gets to his feet, finds a smile, and takes Jesso's hand, 'I'll see you again, Jesso – give my regards to your wife.'

At the door Jesso calls him. Khalil turns. The other makes a peak of his hand above his eyes to stop the window sun from dazzling.

'Yes, Jesso?'

'I think that someone does know. Has answers.'

'Allah has.'

'Or perhaps one of His faithful.'

Khalil nods. Says he must hurry, look at the time, Daoud will think he is lost.

10

A few strides from Jesso's the roaring of engines causes Khalil to draw up short. He squints hard – recognizes the racket – he doesn't like to walk the street when the metal dinosaurs come this way. Old terrors, Zarifa calls them.

They come into his field of vision then, chasing their own din, a pair of Israeli half-tracks grinding along the street, escorting a truck convoy of soldiers on changeover from the hilltop compounds that are strung along the south Lebanese skyline like charms on a bracelet – charms that are too few and too distantly spaced to have the desired effect.

The guerrillas attack and attack and daily are becoming more brazen in their efforts.

Khalil admires their persistence – it is like watching a fly hovering around a wasp, buzzing to try and irritate it to death, or at the very least have it move on.

They are certainly giving the Israelis enough dead for thought. The difference in might and numbers, he often tells his familiar customers, is minimized by this – the Hezbollah are well trained, focused and are prepared to and indeed want to die for their cause. They don't want fast cars, holidays, money, women or career prospects – their minds are uncluttered. The Israeli soldier values his life – enjoys discos and sipping at cappuccinos under café awnings watching scantily clad ladies, wants to own a car and his own place – he wants to live, enjoy life. That is the difference between the soldiers of the two armies. But – always a but, the day the young Israeli decides to be like the Hezbollah is the day the wasp turns and stings.

The tan coloured half-tracks, armoured personnel carriers, rumble closer. It appears to him that the engines growl excessively for the low speed at which they travel.

Intimidatingly – typical Israeli posturing – bellicose bastards.

Road wheels revolve on the steel tracks, the tracks biting into the asphalt – the noise, the smell of churning dust and diesel smoke, the soldiers wearing relieved faces now that they are almost home. Time to live and go wild, because in Lebanon, in Lebanon you just don't know if you're going to come out the way you went in. Young soldiers in baggy olive uniforms all smiles.

Suddenly, one of them sitting atop the leading half-track,

legs dangling over the armoured side skirting, raises his Galil rifle and points it at Khalil. The moment passes – the half-track lurches on – the soldier glancing back to show a smile – no offence – a joke – conqueror to serf.

Khalil shuffles on past Dahab's and stops outside his shop. He had intended going for a meal but spent longer in Jesso's than intended.

So it has come about.

His wasp turns to sting.

If his father were missing would he search for him, after fifteen years?

Yes.

You didn't look for your brother.

He is not my father. And how could I have – where do jackals bury their bones?

Still. Of your blood. Should you not have at least tried?

I will be with him soon enough.

This quietens the voice.

He stands at the door of his locked shop. Daoud is unaware of the tired eyes that take him in.

He is sitting on a rug playing with a black and white kitten about six weeks old. Now and then Daoud picks the kitten up and looks into its eyes. He talks to the cat, is tender with it, tickles and engages in finger boxing with the small paws.

The boy had been out front earlier – clues of sunflower

seeds and orange peel on the ground. He would have gone indoors when he heard the half-tracks coming.

This is a time when Daoud does not want to think about his brother – this is a time for playing with his kitten. Daoud lifts a finger and admonishes his pet for touching his G Shock – the watch almost hanging off the boy's hand must be a terrible temptation for a kitten not long past the stage of chasing shadows.

Khalil raps on the door. Daoud responds and draws the bolts. Smiles.

'What time is it, Daoud?' He points to his own watch.

The boy squints, '13.45.'

'Which is?'

'Don't know.'

'Is it so that you can only read the time sometimes?'

'My brain gets lazy, Khalil. It has been lazy all day.'

Khalil asks him, ruffles his hair, 'Are you hungry?'

'Sure.'

'Sure?'

'Yes.'

'And your kitten?'

Nods.

'Well, we'll leave the shop closed until we've eaten – will you go to George's and get roast chicken and hummus, fresh bread – tell him they're for me – he knows the way I like things cooked.'

Daoud says, 'No problemo, Khalil.'

Spittle on the boy's lips reveals his hunger. Khalil proffers a $5 bill and tells him to let his mother know where he is going.

As Khalil closes the door after the boy, the kitten starts to fight with Khalil's bare toes.

'*Imshi*, go on – find a mouse, there are enough of them about.'

But the kitten persists.

'Little rogue – come here.'

As he bends forward the pain flares – loud, angry and aggressive – it is as though someone has taken a knife to his flesh and is cutting away a rib. Vigorously, he rubs the affected spot. Struggles his way to his chair and sits down, the hurting loud becoming louder. Features tightening, per-spiration coming in thick beads to his forehead. And then, abruptly, there is relief.

The eye of the storm.

Inhales a deep breath and slowly exhales, the gnawing is present but low key.

The boy is back.

Khalil lets him in and makes for the kitchen, the kitten toying with Daoud's feet.

'What's its name?' Khalil says, putting the strips of chicken breast on paper plates and tearing the pitta bread in half.

'Cutie.'

Khalil frowns to smother a smile.

'Nice name,' he says.

'Second name is Xena.'

'Cutie Xena,' Khalil says, making for the table, indicating with a nod for Daoud to join him.

'Yes – I like Xena – do you? Warrior Princess – she's on the TV.'

'I know – she's very strong, isn't she?'

'Uh-huh.'

'But what if Cutie is a man – would you like to be called Cutie?'

'No. She's a girl cat.'

'Sure, you're sure?'

'Yes, Khalil – I looked, she has two holes.'

'Daoud?'

'Yes?'

'When people ask you if Cutie is a boy or girl kitten don't say she has two holes.'

'Why not?'

'It's not polite. And a businessman has always got to be polite.'

'O.K.'

After the meal he sends the boy home, paid up with his two dollars, and opens the shop. Cutie is gone too, with new red flea collar and tinkle bell. Almost five in the afternoon, too early for the troops in the HQ to begin filtering through the French Wadi Gate and the South Gate, near Mingi Street Hotel. The door is open, the bait is cast.

The MP will drop in this evening. There is nothing surer. But he can't keep avoiding O'Driscoll.

What does he say to him?

Little.

As little as possible.

Deny.

What is there to deny? You were there – yes – you arrived in time to see the soldiers hanging, the last kicks coming from the Irishman. You can tell him what you saw. But it won't be enough.

He will want to know where the body is buried.

And, Khalil, you can tell him, can't you? You can tell him where his father lies. In Lebanon it is blood that matters, in some shape or form it always comes down to blood.

Meaning?

Meaning, Khalil? Does the loss of a loved one not drive people – some people – *madjnoun*? Blood, family, is all.

Zarifa drops in about seven and makes him coffee. By that time he has seen off three customers – a Swede called Pers Larsson bought a Casio electric typewriter, two Fijians spent more time than money buying two Swatch watches, cutting him back a dollar in price which satisfied him and them. They saved a dollar and he didn't have to drop the two more he would have had they pushed him for another minute. Bargaining – it makes him forget – it makes him live for the moment – best price for you, my friend.

One of the Fijians had about 6,000 Lebanese pounds, a little short of $4, and bought a tin of *maamul* patisseries, white biscuits stuffed with walnut paste. Said he was going to church service that evening – would Khalil like to come? He will meet him at the gate. Come along. Khalil said he would be there – nothing surer he will be there – a little late in my life for conversion, though – don't you think?

The Fijian smiled and said, 'Inshallah.'

All dollar. Once Zarifa accused him of being in love with the dollar – he was all dollar and not all family. He should be into family. He told her to leave him alone. That this was a bad day for her to start on at him.

The dollar.

What's the currency in Heaven? Or in Hell? His father used to say that you can't bring money to the grave. He meant its power, of course. The currency you bring with you is love and the tears your loved ones weep for you, their prayers, that is what you bring before Allah's throne, His bank.

He smiles – ah, the hereafter won't be so bad – not if he's going to a place where he can add and subtract, talk profit and shop. Not so bad, at all.

Ah, Khalil – but you have an overdraft to contend with –

quite a sizable one, too. It's going to take a lot of burnt mint leaves, a lot of prayers from your loved ones to set your account even half right. How long will Zarifa live, and Adeeba? After they have gone is there anyone who will care enough to whisper your name to Allah?

'Khalil – you haven't been listening to me – have you? You haven't heard a word that I've said – sitting there like a fool grinning to himself.'

He shakes his head, 'Sorry – I was far away.'

'What were you thinking about?'

'Angels – I was playing with angels.'

'Haven't you time enough for that?'

In almost the same breath Zarifa apologizes.

'A woman's mouth is her greatest failing,' he says.

Zarifa sighs, 'Adeeba had a call from Ossie today.'

'Yes?'

'He is putting on his old devil charm – wants her back.'

'And?'

'I think she will go back – she says that she won't but her eyes tell me differently.'

'To being one of his wives?'

Although a Muslim may marry three wives it was something never considered by Khalil, not even in jest, for Zarifa could be a jealous woman and read into things that were not written.

Zarifa has a brother who married a second wife and when

he brought her home, his first wife refused to let her into the house. So he divorced his second wife, paid her $5,000 in compensation and these days avoids her village as though its each and every door is crossed with an X. Even when he had been injured in a car accident he asked the ambulance driver to take the long way round to the hospital. She had put the death eye on him – the curse of a woman disenfranchised of the fine house and new relative splendour she had thought was hers. A long way from a bed in a grim room with four sisters, one of whom was mildly retarded. Another brother, Adfal, works in northern Lebanon, a loner, an administrator of an asylum. Khalil's memory of him is scant. He remembers how dangerous he looked, his intelligent eyes, his quick smile that held a glint of cruelty.

'Yes – she wants to go back and embrace him – add to her collection of black eyes and broken bones.'

'And when his new wife is pregnant she will – so messy, so . . .'

Khalil shakes his head.

'So, what will you do, Khalil?'

He is weary. What can he do? He realizes that Zarifa is pushing his illness to the back of her mind – his death won't happen until it happens.

'What do you suggest?'

'Talk to her.'

'She won't listen to me.'

'She will.'

'What do I say? Zarifa – only the obvious – she mustn't go back to him. Not if she wants to have a life.'

'London.'

'She won't go there.'

'She will. Nada – she always liked our Adeeba.'

Nada is Zarifa's youngest sister.

Khalil nods. It's possible – a gentle nudge and Adeeba might visit her Aunt Nada.

'I will try – in the morning when she comes down to take over the shop.'

'You're staying here tonight?'

'Didn't we agree – every second night?'

'Yes – but—'

'Ah, Zarifa, a man needs to build up his strength.'

She blushes.

It's starting though – the drive to take him home and keep him there. In a couple of weeks why not? Adeeba could be in England and ah, yes, he's tired. Has he the energy, the time left to confront his demons, soothe his conscience before . . .?

He sips at his coffee and goes to speak but the noise from Dahab's is loud – an indistinct voice at first but when its intensity rises and the profanities thicken he recognizes it as Aziz's. He makes to rise but Zarifa caps his hand with hers.

'No – you must not interfere.'

Slowly he removes her hand, meets her eyes, and says, 'You don't understand, Zarifa, I have stood back when I shouldn't have – I have always stood back when I shouldn't have.'

He goes to the door.

11

Khalil notices the scuff marks left by the half-tracks on the asphalt, the slight breeze that like Zarifa's words try to push him back from entering Dahab's, the scent of the flowers from the hanging baskets Dahab had watered a short time ago – cuttings of wild mountain flowers snipped by Zarifa in Baalbek the last time she visited home.

Aziz's silver Mercedes – how many cars does he own? – fronts Dahab's door, bird dirt on the roof and bonnet and on parts of the windscreen out of reach of the wash and wipers.

Drawing your car up close to a person's door is like sticking your nose in her face.

Aziz's voice touches his ears from behind a wooden door.

'Your mother is a cow!

'You are a cow.'

'A whore!'

'A stupid fucking bitch!'

'You cunt!'

'A fucking bloodsucker!'

'Your mother and father were thieves!'

Things crash. Where is Dahab's voice in the face of this raging storm? Lost.

You're waiting, Khalil, still hesitating – you know what should be done, what needs to be said and done. Like you knew all those years ago but you stayed quiet, did nothing. What is it with you, Khalil? Are you just full of piss and wind?

Khalil opens the door. The hinges squeak, the door falls shut behind him. A rerun of *M*A*S*H* is on TV. Corporal Klinger in a dress and wide brim hat. Through a curtain door not fully drawn he sees Daoud sitting on the edge of his bed, kitten on his lap, feet crossed, looking straight ahead, shoulders raised.

Aziz has his back to Khalil, falling silent when he follows Dahab's eyes over his shoulder. Khalil is acutely aware of the revolver Aziz nurses in the small of his back. Aziz half-turns, keeping an eye and ear on each of them.

He is lean and short with gelled black hair and a trimmed moustache. His lower lip a pencilled outline, the upper thin as though stretched. A former SLA officer, he is one of Kasni's cohorts, a strong-arm debt collector, smuggler, drug dealer. Only Allah knows what else he does in the shade.

'I thought the TV too loud, but it seems it is you who is too loud, Aziz.'

'Get out, get the fuck out of here!'

'I think it is you who should leave.'

Aziz turns square on Khalil, pointing, 'This my fucking home and my fucking family, now get out of here before I fucking throw you out.'

The rage in his eyes is a rage Khalil has seen before. In some people it is a silent rage. They remain quiet, accepting their lot, spirits quenched. Apathy, inner anger, a sense of futility, of hopelessness. Rages like Aziz's burn with an intense hatred at anything that stands between them and their immediate goal, explosions that sooner rather than later spend themselves or are spent.

'You would hurt me, an old man?'

Khalil sees the weal under Dahab's left eye, where Aziz's hand has freshened the wound.

'Get out!'

'Your son is listening, and probably the boy you buried, too.'

Aziz starts for Khalil, Dahab tugging at his blue shirt, 'Please Aziz, don't, don't.'

Without looking at her he shakes her off and Khalil braces himself for the blow. But he doesn't blink.

'I will have you shot,' Khalil whispers, 'I will spend a fortune to see it done.'

In that instant he has some hold on Aziz and presses forward his advantage, 'Do you think the village has no Hezbollah? Every morning you check your car you are being watched. Everything you do they know.'

Aziz trembles with the effort of confining his rage.

'I am dying, Aziz, do what you want with me, I don't care – it will save me a lot of suffering.'

'You have no right to be here.'

'You have no right to be striking your wife, terrorizing your son – you are the Mukhtar of this village, a leader – is this how you see yourself, Aziz?'

'Leave us alone, Khalil. I know people who can hurt those you leave behind.'

'Mine know that – but they sent me in here to warn you – it is they who make the threat. I am here because I do not want to die less than a man in their eyes.'

In a flash Dahab is behind Aziz, snatching the revolver from his back. Steps back, pointing.

He laughs, 'Shoot me, go on, do it.'

Khalil says, 'No, Dahab – don't. Don't.'

The fool can't see that she wants to kill him so much. He should shut up. He's sneering – don't sneer at her.

'Dahab, think of Daoud – think of him.'

'She didn't think of our other boy! Bitch.'

Dahab squeezes the trigger. The retort is loud, smoky. Aziz staggers back gripping his shoulder, blood oozing between his fingers. He doubles over, straightens up, the shock in his eyes surrendering to bemusement.

Dahab lowers the revolver and then raises it. Aziz backs away, loosening his hand, fidgeting for his keys in his jeans pocket, the blood seeping through the short sleeve of his T-shirt.

'Dahab,' pleads Khalil.

Hinges squeak, car engine starts, is revved away. Khalil catches the scent of cordite in his nostrils as he walks towards Dahab. Is this what happens when you interfere?

Worsen the situation? If he hadn't walked in then Dahab would have taken the beating she is used to taking. Aziz would have had her against her will. All this would not have happened.

Zarifa breezes through, fear in her eyes and her mouth hanging open, showing the new teeth she bought in Beirut, wearing them even though they chafe her gums.

'Khalil?'

'I'm all right.'

There is blood on the concrete floor, smeared where Aziz had walked. Khalil extends his hand and nods for Dahab to give him the revolver. She places it on his palm.

Zarifa wraps her arm around her shoulders, 'Come inside the back, come on.'

Dahab cries, sobs hard. Daoud runs to her, calls her Mamma.

Khalil says, 'Zarifa, bring them to the village – I will take care of things here.'

Zarifa breathes, 'O.K.'

Zarifa has just left when Jesso and a couple of others show their faces. They heard the shot. Jesso is armed with a sawn-off shotgun.

Khalil, panting, tells them what happened.

'I know that mad bastard, Khalil – he won't let her get away with this. I know him.'

'No – he knows now that once she has struck out she will do the same again.'

'She should have killed him.'

'Not in front of the boy – this was just a cry for him to leave them alone.'

Jesso shakes his head.

Khalil hands him the revolver, 'Will you see him?'

'Yes, I'll see the fuck.'

'Give him this,' he empties the chamber, spilling the rounds onto his palm, 'and these. Tell him not to remember so much what Dahab has done but what I have said.'

'What did you say?'

'Ask him. Just convince him that it's as true as the hole in his arm.'

Adeeba arrives about an hour and a half later. By then Khalil has mopped up the blood and squeezed the mop's head of blood into a sluice channel at the back of Dahab's garden. He plucked the head of the round from a timber upright close to the door. He had thought the bullet had passed through the tin – there are many holes in the corrugated walls where nails had fallen out, but it was lodged an inch inside the wood and sat there like a worm too exhausted to burrow any farther.

It didn't seem right to leave the round in there, looking out at people. It also gave him something to do, to take his mind off things.

Dahab's yard was all a clutter. A slatted fence and some rose bushes served as a flimsy partition between gardens, a gap exists which Daoud uses to access Khalil's garden, coming to his back door with his timid little rapping.

The view from Dahab's garden was different from his own. He took in the houses on the western hill. He saw his own, and beyond that, out of view, was Aziz's new place. Beside Jesso's an old camel, the colour of red earth with the sun on its back, chewed on shrubs, thick lips moving slowly, contemptuously. Khalil had often heard him bellowing but had never actually set eyes on him.

'They are O.K.,' Adeeba says, looking about at the squalor and poverty of Dahab's house.

'O.K.?' he says, putting his hand through his robe's side opening and surfacing a pack of Gitane smokes from his slacks pocket.

'The boy is quiet – just sitting watching TV.'

'He shuts himself away – I saw him doing it at his brother's funeral, looking at the coffin entering the ground but at the same time he was far away. And Dahab?'

'Dazed.'

Her soft features ripple with concern.

'You should sit down, Papa, take it easy – I have locked up the shop.'

Had he left it open? Careless. Messing about with a bullet in timber and a splinter in his finger while his shop lay unattended. He had assumed Zarifa had closed it up.

'All she talks about is the soldiers coming to collect her laundry and drop more in – she wants to be here for them.'

'She needs their clothes so she can eat.'

'Not tonight she doesn't or the next – I will leave a note on the door.'

Khalil pulls on his cigarette. Bites on his lower lip. He walks into Daoud's room.

A made up bed, crinkled duvet where Daoud had been sitting, a rug on the concrete floor, posters of Manchester United teams and Ryan Giggs running with the ball at his toes. A steel bedside locker with a model Spitfire warplane on top, a stack of comics on shelves, his G Shock watch hanging from a nail, above it a photograph of himself and the boy at a barbecue held in the UN compound last year. Khalil can't remember it being taken. It had been a good day. He would have had his photograph taken with a lot of people. No one other than Daoud has a photograph of him in his room. He would bet his life savings on that – of all the houses and shops in Naqoura and Mingi Street, no one would have a photograph of him pinned up.

None of Daoud's dead brother, of his mother, or Aziz – you couldn't call him a father. A swell of pride in him that he knows is quite ridiculous for an old man to feel, but still can't keep from feeling.

A clean room. A few toy soldiers, a football, a skateboard with broken wheels, a variety of baseball caps that Daoud occasionally wears peak to neck. No window – he should have a window. The room is too dark. Always the naked bulb has to be on, dangling from its cord, a miniature night and day sun. Stubs of candle in brass holders for when the sun blows. A lighter beside it – the boy fears the dark, fears the noise of the wind, the noise of the half-tracks, the sound of gunfire, a cracking hand, the grunts of his father in his mother's room.

He hears Adeeba turning away some soldiers. A few moments later she calls him.

'In here,' she says, when he has not arrived quickly enough for her liking.

He knows what a woman's bedroom is like. Hesitates outside the curtain.

'Papa?'

He enters. The room is larger than Daoud's. A double

bed with a green velvet bedhead, Persian rugs, a dresser with a rectangular mirror cracked in several places. No woman should tolerate having to look at herself in a cracked mirror. Above the dresser is a cork noticeboard with photographs – of Daoud, and her dead boy, Sami.

Conscription. Most parents railed against their children joining the militia so effectively that the Israelis introduced conscription when their bribes failed. Sami was a quiet boy who kept to himself and couldn't understand why his parents would be so keen for him to turn a rifle on his own Muslim kind. It was all right for the likes of Jesso for he was a Christian and the civil war had been between Muslim and Christian.

There are laundry baskets with waterfalls of clothes along one side of the room and arrayed on the bed are neatly folded piles of clothes tied with string, with names crudely scrawled on paper.

Harry.

Ivors.

Timmy.

Pers.

Mike.

'Adeeba, why did you call me in here?'

'Look.'

She points at a fluffy little thing shivering in a corner by a basket.

'Cutie,' Khalil says.

'The boy asked me to get her – she slipped from his arms when he went to his mother. You know I don't like cats.'

'I'll take him – will you open up the shop? I'll be down later.'

'I can stay the night.'

'No, it's O.K. – there's someone coming to see me – if he comes tell him to wait, that I won't be long.'

Khalil strokes the kitten, puts his finger between its neck and flea collar to check that it isn't too tight.

'Adeeba, before you go – London – I think you should go visit Aunt Nada.'

'I—'

'Your mother asked me to advise you . . .'

'I will go, yes, I think I would like to visit her.'

'You understand if you go back to Ossie you will have no life worth calling a life?'

'Yes.'

'There is someone else for you – I hope you find each other.'

She nods and leaves the room with her head slightly bowed.

Zarifa is right.

It is in Adeeba's mind to return to her husband.

12

Khalil lowers the kitten onto the rear seat and eases the car door shut. A pleasant evening, the sun starting its fall. A few metres along the road the kitten climbs all over him, four white paws on his shoulder, ears raised, eyes taking in the scenery – Khalil edges to the verge and puts the kitten in the boot. He drives the length of the street, a little beyond the hotel, and swings to the right, wheels crunching the pebbles on the semicircle of fine white sand, car facing seawards.

Alighting he walks a short distance before descending a trail between scrub to the skinny shoreline. Out from the strip of stony shore gentle waves wash over grey tabletop rocks, surfaces as smooth as polished bronze.

He steps stones to the last one, the waves a shushing melody over its mesa-like peak.

Khalil wears chinos and a shirt underneath but as summer creeps forward he will abandon the robe. The long garment has become his favourite protection against the draughts that pervade his shop and pass through his bones.

The sun is an orb of fire on the horizon, touching the ocean and then sinking until no longer visible.

Darkness begins to set in.

Around here, this spot, some years ago, four Palestinians landed in a rubber dinghy and climbed the same trail Khalil now embarks. The sand clinging to his wet feet and sandals, irritating a small cut on his little toe.

They came from Ar Rashidiyah south of Tyre, near the orange groves he and his father worked. Early morning, after first light, the first Unifil joggers left camp to run the 6 km to the border, the first two taken hostage and brought into an old shack belonging to Habib who wasn't at home, busy dying in Najib Hospital.

Khalil knew the soldiers, the previous evening one had visited his shop and bought an alarm clock. Khalil remembered because he asked for one that repeats and all Khalil had left was his own, new, that he sold for a dollar above the going rate.

The SLA from their border checkpoint had spotted the hostage taking and mowed the shed walls with persistent machine-gun fire, killing all inside. No mercy – a concept left unconsidered.

Khalil regrets ever selling him the clock. Yes, the soldier would surely have bought another elsewhere on the street, but perhaps he might not have. And if he hadn't then perhaps he would have woken a little later than usual for his training run . . .

Ands and Ifs.

If Yusef had lived then his mother would not have turned *madjnoun*.

He reverses onto the road and noses the car towards the street. His mind a little clearer now, still that sickly feeling in his throat and the gnawing in his stomach and in his heart the uncertainty as to whether or not his interference in the argument had been wise and in Dahab's and Daoud's long-term best interests.

It is dark by the time he reaches his place. Strange how he regards his shop as home and his house as just a place.

The helium streetlights are on, attracting moths that ping against the glass and bats that veer away from a collision at the last moment. He sets the kitten loose and watches her scamper to the nearest shrub. His feet squelch along the ochre flags by the side of the house. Before entering the kitchen he pulls his robe over his head and pegs it to a nail set under a hanging basket. Uses the garden hose to rinse the sand from his feet and then his sandals, leaving them standing upright against the wall to dry like two wide boys full of arrack, and drying his feet in a towel Zarifa keeps on a roller behind the kitchen door. Finds sober flip-flops in a press.

Zarifa doesn't like to see him wearing a robe. She says next thing he'll be wearing a fez like his Turkish grandfather in that sepia photograph. A man to whom Khalil bears a striking resemblance. A gaunt man with deep-set eyes and a thick moustache who fought in World War I at Gallipoli and Akko as a cavalryman.

The acts of bravery – dying men who died trying to help other dying men. Men who cowered on their knees, covering their heads, crying for mercy, but answered only by a single bullet to the back of the neck.

Father said his father was never right in the head after the war. Outwardly he was the same but his eyes were different, a crescent of blood in the whites.

Daoud smiles when he sees his kitten. He has the fresh look of a boy recently bathed.

Zarifa and Dahab sit on the long sofa, a tea tray on the coffee table in front of them, a plate of Ritz crackers.

'Thanks, Khalil.'

'It's O.K.'

He nods at the two women, pours himself tea and takes to the armchair across from them.

Dahab is grey, still dazed.

'Will he live?' she asks of no one in particular.

'Yes – an arm wound – I should think so,' Khalil says.

'I am dead.'

Daoud is listening so Khalil doesn't wish to speak. The child is playing with his kitten but listening to the adults talking at the same time, the way children do.

Dahab squeezes the tissue she holds – wrings it. Zarifa sighs, rubs Dahab's shoulder, looks at Khalil as though to say isn't it terrible to see another person suffering, and to ask can he not lift her sorrow.

How?

Hadn't he brought things to a head?

Made things worse?

'I'm sorry Dahab, I should not have interfered.'

Khalil burns within. He had tried to help. He didn't think it would end up like this, with Aziz in hospital and an accusing silence from Dahab. And Zarifa will start at him as soon as she gets a free moment. Hadn't she told him not to interfere?

Why didn't he listen?

He had done but had chosen to ignore her.

A delayed response – for he wasn't going into Dahab's, he was heading to a pair of olive trees to try and prevent a hanging, to raise a kicking man's feet and have his neck and hands untied.

He shouldn't have bothered.

Confused.

That lost evening he had failed to do the right thing. What

would have happened had he cut in and shouted above the madness, 'Stop!'?

That word might not have had much effect. A pissdrop on hot desert sands. If he had said it and then woven his way past onlookers to the front, would that action have had any effect? If.

The moon was a round scar in the sky, the murmuring of the crowd, the silent baying for blood – the men's deaths appeared to have been written in stone before the cursed event actually happened.

He saw good men turn and walk away, heads lowered, while he stayed, transfixed.

And in the silent aftermath, with the falling away of many, he was left there with three others, and called over to help take down the swaying corpses. Yes, then he could move, when called.

And they beckoned him like they would have done a friend, an ally – almost with affection. He was part of them, with them, had partaken, as Jesso might say, of the same communion host.

Khalil sips at his tea.

Daoud says, 'Khalil, I might take a few days off work.'

'O.K.'

'You won't fire me?'

'No – I'll mark you down in my book as being out sick, with pay.'

Daoud smiles, pushes his G Shock up his arm, returns to his comic, but his kitten wants to play, snatching at his toes with her pink paws then scampering away.

Khalil takes laboured steps towards the kitchen and sits in at the table listening to the radio, drawing on a cigarette. He massages his temples, closes his eyes and breathes deeply.

He needs to discuss things with Zarifa. His bank account, his savings. Things a widow needs to know.

It is hard to envisage that he is so close to the time when the shadow of the Moorish keep will fall across his resting place, that the sun will fall into the sea from its winter angle, that the smell of kerosene and the feel of a crisp dollar in his fingers will be ghost memories of his life.

An afterlife?

Can't see it from here.

Will he have thoughts?

Will he miss Life?

Will he ache inside? His belly burn? Dispense phlegm from his lungs? Have a desire to make love? Repent?

Surely not? Surely these things will be of the past? Death denies you access to the living. Is dying another rebirth? Old sins buried, new ones to be made?

Allah!

Has hidden Himself from the world.

Why?

Show Yourself.

Let me know that it's not over when I draw my last breath and that it is a change of world, and death is like a gear in a car, something you must engage.

An anger consumes him as he swallows pills.

Dust to dust. Ashes to ashes – that taken from the earth must return.

Business is business – Allah – let's talk business, for I am a businessman. Not a religious one. I am sorry, but I do not like the zealousness of my religious brethren, so I don't visit the mosque as often as I should. In fact, seldom has become never. Let me talk with You on my level for I cannot aspire to Yours.

It is a long time since I faced Mecca and prayed. The last time I prayed hard was after the heart attack, when I turned my father's prayer beads so incessantly that it must have irritated You. I prayed because I did not want to feel that sharp piercing pain in my chest again, and while now the pain I endure is bad, becoming more prolonged, it is at least being measured out in a way that I can handle – it is not excruciating. Yet.

I would like to avoid excruciating pain – that is not to say I don't deserve it.

I ask forgiveness; for malice done, for evil thoughts, for occasions of lust, for anything that I have done to cause You offence, intentionally and unintentionally.

For having no faith.

I pray because I want to believe and because the alternative if You are not real is too frightening to comprehend. Be real.

I have a problem.

Do I help the Irishman find his father, tell him everything I know? Break the oath I made on that awful night? Until tonight I thought my mind had been made up – I was going to help. But now – well, You saw what happened tonight. You know.

He grows aware of a presence. The air appears to shift as though making way – a crowd parting to let a dignitary through.

'Khalil?'

Opens his eyes, 'Daoud?'

'There is a call on your mobile – Adeeba says that someone has called to see you.'

He takes the mobile from Daoud but Adeeba has hung up.

'Thanks, Daoud.'

The small boy doesn't stir. He moves a hand up and down his opposite arm, fingernails lightly ploughing white marks on his olive skin.

'The mosquitoes are biting, Daoud, come with me into the sitting room.'

'Will you kill my father?'

'Kill your father?'

'Yes, before he kills me and my mother.'

'He won't kill—'
'He said he will. He's always saying that he will.'
The boy's eyes are large and pleading.
A boy not yet turned eight asking for blood.
Allah?

13

In the shop Adeeba serves a Polish soldier.

'*Ahlan wa Sahlan*,' the soldier greets Khalil, smiling.

He reeks of vodka, small eyes merry.

'*Allah ma'ak*.'

A brace of French soldiers duck in and then out in search of a lost comrade. The Irishman is at the end of the shop feigning interest in a selection of water pipes, carries a black wallet folder that hugs his hip.

Adeeba, after the Pole leaves, says, 'Car keys, Papa, please.'

'Here, Adeeba.'

Her puzzled stare travels from Khalil to O'Driscoll and back again. She senses the current, the charged air, its expectancy.

'I'll see you in the morning, Papa – there is fresh coffee made.'

'Thanks—'

Khalil sees Adeeba out. Closes and bolts the door after her. Sets the shop sign to read 'We're Closed'.

'We should move out the back, it's better, the shop gets cold later on.'

The other nods. He is wirily built, black hair freshly cut, eyes that are the blue of the sea in certain lights. He wears desert shoes, navy jeans and a red sleeveless shirt. A light film of hair on his forearm cobwebs a tattoo of the Irish tricolour flag.

Khalil draws back the curtain, thumbs the lights, and indicates O'Driscoll to the table.

He follows him in with the coffee pot and miniature cups.

'So, Sergeant, what can I do for you?'

O'Driscoll pats his shirt pocket, takes out his Lucky Strikes and shows the pack to Khalil who after a moment's hesitation plucks a cigarette. Khalil also accepts a flame from O'Driscoll's disposable lighter. Pours coffee – grateful to have the flowing noise interrupt the awkward silence, getting the preliminaries, perhaps what will turn out to be the best of the niceties done with.

'Good, you're being direct. We should get where I want to bring you very quickly.'

The Irishman's soft voice is scored with steel.

'That is so if I want to go with you, Sergeant.'

The room begins to fill with blue cigarette smoke. The coffee is cold and sweet.

A chill pervades.

'Arrack?' Khalil suggests.

'If you like.'

'I ask if you would like.'

'Yes.'

Khalil opens a cupboard and draws two glasses and a bottle of Ksara arrack.

'This has a mild liquorice flavour.'

'I've drunk arrack before.'

'Yes, I forgot, you've been in Lebanon before, good.'

Khalil sits, 'Now let's get to the point, Sergeant.'

'It's about my father.'

Khalil nods non-committally.

'He and an American major were hanged not far from here fifteen years ago.'

'I remember.'

'On June the eight – fifteen years next week to be precise.'

'Why have you come to me? How can I help?'

Is there a resemblance between the man and his son? It is hard to tell. He remembers more of the man's kicking feet than his face. Terror had contorted his features.

A shudder steals through him, making water of his insides. So clear the image – torchlight revealed the grotesque sight – pale gossamer features, eyes popping, his nose hanging on to his face by a thin stretch of skin, teeth bared a little, enough to see the slivers from his last meal between his teeth, top of a Snickers wrapper peeping out of his shirt's breast pocket, a silver crucifix on a silver chain winking back. Snapped the torch blind on Sourb's instruction. He said he didn't like to see the dead grinning.

'I believe you were there that night.'

'What makes you believe that?'

'I read the UN report compiled back then – your name was listed along with others who passed through the Fijian checkpoint that night on the Qana road.'

'There are many who used that road.'

'I know – but you know your people.'

'Meaning?'

'Meaning?' O'Driscoll pulls a face, 'For instance if I'm heading towards a village and I'm not sure of the way and stop to ask an old man – well, he might give me directions or he might say I should not go there. He won't tell me why I should not go there. But only a fool doesn't read the warning. It is the same with people who made the statements, they gave names without actually telling the investigators why they were giving these names.'

Khalil nods.

Yes, the investigators called to his home and he denied that he had been anywhere near that location. Lots of visits, lots of questions. In the end he refused even to discuss things with them. He had done nothing. They were persecuting him. Had put his shop out of bounds to the soldiers – punishing an innocent man, he lamented. A Norwegian MP by the name of Borge told him he was not innocent but silent. Stuck his forefinger in his face.

If Borge had not had to return home at the end of his tour of his duty he might have got results. His tongue was a hard tool that unearthed truths.

Time blew its mists and the soldiers filtered back to his shop. Khalil had nothing to hide, they said. The Irish breathed that he was, 'Sound. A sound man.'

O'Driscoll's fingers tap dance on the black folder. Satisfied he has Khalil's attention he opens the flap, pushes across photographs.

Of a smiling man in army uniform, another with a boy of about twelve – ah yes, the resemblance. Striking. The man in a suit, cigarette fastened in the corner of his mouth, the pavement he stands on wet, puddles along the kerbside, a shore blocked with leaves and sweet papers. Outside a hotel or a cinema, which? Cinema. The Round Tower Cinema.

Family photograph of a father and mother, two boys, three girls – all pretty, smiling, in a studio.

'That's my mother, she died last December, on Christmas Eve. She got the cancer bad and quick.'

'My brother is in the States, has dual citizenship, works with the FBI in the computer end. My three sisters are all married and working, all have children.'

Khalil freshens their glasses.

'My father missed out on all these occasions.'

'A lot of people do.'

'Yes, but not because they were hung from a tree.'

His fingers push papers towards Khalil.

'Case notes from the investigation – you'll see your name there, prominent along with others – most of them dead, now.'

'Rumour and innuendo.'

'I don't think so – do you believe in Allah?'

'Of course. But not always, no.'

'Aren't the origins of most religions grounded in rumour and innuendo?'

'Perhaps – so, my friend, every spark comes from a fire, is that so?'

'I think so – yes, in this case – and I'm not your friend – none of your shop talk, please – I am not here to bargain you down on a cheap radio.'

'What do you want from all this, want of me?'

O'Driscoll leans forward, 'I want my father's remains. I want to bring him home. I want to bury him with my mother.'

'It happened so long ago.'

'Will you help me?'

Help? Allah, how do I help without telling him everything?

Skimp on the truth? The truth is brutal, too brutal. If he is going the road of truth then he must travel its whole length, every turn and twist. And yet, is the decision to travel that route his to make?

'I want my father back – and I want all the details – spare me nothing. The full story.'

Can he read minds, this man?

'Why now, after all this time?'

O'Driscoll lowers his head. Khalil sees a small white scar at his temple, an island of flesh in the black sea of his hair.

'Sometimes I dream. I hear his voice calling me. We're playing soccer in the park – passing the ball to each other. He kicks it over my head and I run for it and when I turn about to pass it to him he isn't there. It is a real day, in the background a train is slowing on its approach to the station. The grass a vivid green and too long for football. My father's face as clear as yours is to me – there with me one moment, gone the next. Forever gone. And there is another reason.'

'I'm listening, my . . .'

O'Driscoll's stony-eyed look catches Khalil before he says 'friend'.

'My mother asked me to come to Lebanon and bring him back. The way it was said, when it was said, left no room for discussion, for talk of failure. She talked of bringing him home as though I had only to cross the road and take his hand. You – me – Khalil, we know it isn't so simple. I need you to make it happen.'

Khalil coughs. Pain prods. Out back he spits into the spittoon that usually keeps him company at night.

Drying his mouth he takes up his seat at the table, 'You must excuse me, every so often I must—'

'I understand.'

'I am not a well man – full of poison.'

'I understand that, too.'

'When you were in Lebanon before why didn't – I mean did you not—'

'Investigate then? No. Not beyond talking to a couple of mukhtars – but nothing intensive.'

'Why not?'

'At that time my father wasn't calling me – also the situation on the ground, the fighting, made it impossible to probe. Things are a little quieter, now.'

'For now.'

Khalil frowns, touches his nose, his wart, guards his mouth with his hand as though to prevent words from escaping.

'I'm in the park, Khalil – I can't see him – but I hear him calling me. It's time for him to come home.'

'I—'

'His name was James, people called him Jimmy. They call me Jimmy. You can, too.'

'Have you to report into the compound before the French lock the gates?'

'I have all night. I am in Lebanon for the purpose of finding my father's body – after that, in October, I'm leaving the army – intend opening a shop near to where I live.'

'Where do you live, Jimmy?'

Their eyes meet.

Khalil realizes he is on the road to telling him everything. Relief – it will come before the morning sun rises.

The Sergeant sips at his arrack, chews on his lower lip, 'I'm from Kildare town, it's about twenty-six kilometres from Dublin.'

'I was in Dublin once. Ah, a long time ago. I visited London, Dublin, Cardiff and Glasgow. The year Nelson's Pillar was blown up – how long ago? I was there on that day. My wife, Zarifa, accompanied me. They were good days before the war – I was making a lot of money in Beirut, had a fine shop – we travelled most of Europe, even Israel. I have cousins there, in Akko.'

'I've been to Akko.'

'Ah, see, we have walked in each other's footsteps. Go on, keep talking, don't mind me if I have to spit or take a pill, I'll still be listening.'

'Nice town, Kildare, nice people, not much to do there except booze – a town full of pubs.'

'Yes, I know – I have spoken to others from there – you know Timmy Allen?'

'Yes.'

'Harry Kyle?'

'No.'

'A good man. Gerry Watson – Captain?'

'To see, that's all.'

'They are from Kildare, yes, all of them. You have a round tower there, yes, built by the monks to escape to when the Vikings came. And a rugby club – I played a small bit of rugby in my young days. It is true. Yes, it is – your father, tell me about him.'

'He was from Wexford.'

Khalil knows soldiers who live there but doesn't say a word. It is time to travel the road. His silence is a signal for Jimmy to continue.

'From Boolavogue, a small village. He was a quiet man, the sort who would never set out to cause offence, a kind man, he never hit us. Never lifted his voice. He was rarely ever in bad humour. He was a cook, loved the job – he went out on Saturday nights for a couple of drinks – Saturdays were his favourite day – he would work Sunday rather than a Saturday – on Saturdays he fried for us in the morning and then we wouldn't see him for the whole day. He'd buy his paper and spend a lot of time picking out what horses he was going to back, and then he'd walk for a long distance, across fields during summer and on country roads during winter. He liked to walk. He came out here to earn some extra money. My older brother wanted to go to college and Dad wanted to buy a car – he never had a car, see. Had only learned to drive a few months before he arrived in Lebanon – had been on an army driving course. Don't know how he passed because a friend of his told us he couldn't reverse around corners. He loved driving.

'Mum used to send him newspaper cuttings of car sales. He was on about buying a Volkswagen Beetle. It had to be blue.

'Dad failed at his first attempt to go overseas – you know the Irish, we volunteer, we aren't detailed to serve abroad?'

Khalil nods.

'He had a shadow on his lungs. He was bitterly disap-pointed – then six months later he talked the doctor into letting him go – he had quit smoking after his initial rejec-tion and told the doctor he would start smoking again if he didn't pass him fit.'

He pauses, then continues, 'You see, Khalil, Dad got his warning but went on into the village regardless.'

'Yes, yes, I see.'

'He had less than a week to serve out here when he was killed.'

'I read about that, yes.'

'We were so excited about him coming home. The house

was painted and the garden done. He bought us lovely things – he probably bought something in your shop.'

Possible? Yes. He might have been one of many soldiers who had come in and bought something in those early days, when soldiers were plenty and the trade brisk. Jimmy's voice falters, cracks, 'The army handed over his suitcase and his kitbag, his personal belongings too – the razor blade with some of his whisker shavings, his flip-flops, the photographs he kept pinned to the wall beside his bunk, his fingermarks on them, the letters we wrote to him all bound with elastic, his birthday cards. We buried an empty coffin, you know? Mum thought it would be good therapy for us. She went a little funny, you know, afterwards, in the head.'

Madjnoun.

'Who could blame her?' Jimmy says, more to himself than Khalil.

Khalil coughs and spits into the Frisbee he had taken from the shop. Dabs at his mouth with a tissue.

'It rained that day and the wind was biting – a rage of a day. Opening the ground for it to receive my mother's coffin brought it back home to all of us – standing, looking down, seeing the lie that was my father's coffin – that day, that evening, I got a promise from the Minister of Defence to allow me to conduct this final search for my father's body. Here I am. All roads lead here, to you, Khalil Abbas.'

Khalil nods. Getting to his feet he ignites the kerosene

heater. Reads the gauge – half full, enough to last the night. When he sits down, Jimmy locks his eyes with his.

'Now, it's your turn.'

'I am ready, Sergeant.'

14

The MP Sergeant leans back in his chair and then straightens up, interlocks his fingers under his chin and bipeds his elbows on the table.

Khalil runs his beads through his thumb and forefinger. Where to start?

At the beginning, Khalil – do you know of another place? No.

It is equally important to know where to stop. Are you thinking of telling the whole truth and nothing but the truth, Khalil? Will you, really? Really give something away that's not yours? Giving away something that's not yours is another form of thievery.

You would prefer to be somewhere else, sitting on a different chair in a different room in a different country, about to speak different words to a different man about a different matter. But . . .

Consider this a practice run for you. A chance for some if not total redemption – there can never be a total redemption. You understand – keeper of my soul?

Please, Voice – leave me alone.

'Warts and all, Mister Abbas. Warts and all,' the Sergeant says, his tone frilled with impatience.

'Drink?' Khalil suggests.

'A toast to the beginning of the end, is that it?'

'Just a drink to oil the tongue.'

Khalil wipes his lips. Lips that suddenly feel parched and cracked.

Continues.

'That morning, a Saturday morning, I woke early, feeling good in myself. Watered Zarifa's red roses out back, made coffee. My house on the hill was not even a notion then, so Zarifa and Adeeba lived here with me. You should have seen the Street back then, the life, the vitality, the goodwill – for the first time in a long time we felt safe. A UN camp across from us for security and we also had the SLA patrolling the Street, charging us a tax for the privilege, but we had good money coming in and the sound of gunfire was distant – we were not in its line for a change. A man can get used to living in peace. Gets so he is willing to pay a price for it.

Part of the price is to live among your enemies.

Here, we live close to the dragon's breath, the Israeli border. We see and hear the Israelis roaring down the Street in their half-tracks, their warplanes bombing our country, killing our people. It feels like this, Sergeant; imagine a stranger walking in and around your house at will, knocking your furniture about, slapping your family as you sit upstairs pretending not to notice.

'The stranger sleeps in the same room as you and he leaves you alone to prosper because he needs peace, too – a place to rest his head. A place where he can eat and drink, feel wanted, loved – and yet he is aware that it is a love given to a conqueror. A love due to him for being merciful. Perhaps the most deceitful strain of all loves – ingredients of tolerance, compliance and hatred. A sort of traitor's love – a Judas syndrome.'

Khalil pauses, draws his tongue along his lower lip and then polishes off his arrack.

'The Mukhtar of Yatar Silm was being buried in the afternoon. He and two of his sons had been killed when they attacked an SLA compound. This was a time when such attacks were poorly coordinated and carried out with no real chance of success. Poorly equipped, they were assaults grounded in an indignant rage rather than planned and coherent military operations.

The enemy had night sights and tanks and mines. Now,

these days, the odds have lessened. There are dogs of war abroad, but you know of them, know how the cards to both camps fall evenly. There is a game on, and the winner, listen to me now, Sergeant, will be the Hezbollah. We are not talking if but when.

Others in the Street left for the funeral early. I stayed behind, had not intended going as I had been to the funerals of the two boys earlier that week. Such a waste of young life. This hilltop position they attacked was abandoned a week later by the SLA and the Israelis for a larger fortification on a higher hill – the move had been planned for some time – it highlighted the lack of intelligence the Mukhtar had of the ground – but their anger and indignation was such that perhaps they knew but had been driven to the extent that they no longer cared. But the action made the loss of life appear much more senseless.

In the afternoon business was quiet and Zarifa had been harping on at me to go – you know the way women are – they want you out from under their feet. And I listened to her because I had begun to think that some funerals, like weddings and other important functions, you need to be seen at. And the widow might have thought that I was making a statement by staying away from her husband's funeral. I knew of her, the strange notions she took.

A border of compound fortifications divides us but many here on the Street have relatives – cousins near and distant in villages controlled by the resistance – it is a good idea to show sympathy, to help where it is possible, because a favour rendered is like saving money for a rainy day.

I, too have relatives in villages hereabouts, people I have never seen. I left home when young, after my father died, made for Beirut and worked by day and studied by night. Had everything, Sergeant, then nothing and had to build again. But before I could rebuild I had to ensure my family's safety and so I ended up here, a refugee like others rallying close to the UN flag because it offered some hope. Staying on, putting corrugated roots here and after my first morning spent under this tin shack I went outside and looked at the blue UN flag and the rising sun and this feeling washed over me – that, yes, we would be safe here. And this was a great feeling, because we had nowhere else left to run.

I drove a blue pick-up. It had bald tyres and the seats inside were dirty and showed its guts of foam. It was giving me a lot of trouble, the alternator was running down the battery, but it started with a push and I was on my way.

I drove towards the first checkpoint. You know the one outside Mingi Street, beyond the banana plantation, where the port is, that one. Headed along the road, the sea to my left and the hills to the right. There's a spot about ten kilometres from Mingi Street where you meet a rise, chalk cliffs tower above you to a UN observation post and on the opposite side fall away to foam and rocks – look northeast and you can see Tyre jutting out into the sea like a spill of salt across a table, the sun glancing off the windows on its tall apartment blocks – that's how far back the tailback was – it took almost two hours to pass through the SLA checkpoint's series of swing gates, then a short drive to the UN checkpoint – by the time I reached Yatar Silm it was almost dark. I knew I had missed the funeral but decided to press on, pay my respects and on the way home pull into an orange or tobacco grove, a place where I could expect not to be disturbed, and sleep in the cab.

The village was deserted. Not a soul out and about. They were indoors, most of them.

The widow and her daughters cried when they saw me. Wailed. It was as though they had to do this for me – that they wouldn't have me talking about their house being full of dry eyes. Other women joined in. The widow, a craggy-faced woman, typical mountain stock – poor, toothless, hardened, said if I hurried I might not be too late to help the others.'

Khalil takes in Jimmy's eyes, raises his eyebrows as though to ask if he should continue.

'Go on.'

'The next bit is hard.'

'Do you think I have never imagined what it must have

been like for him? The cold terror that probably had him shitting on himself, the praying he did, the begging – do you think I haven't had nightmares about how he died? That I didn't curse every single fucker that was there and their families? Because by fuck I did, Mister Abbas, you don't realize how fucking hard I cursed the lot of you. Night after night after night.'

'I am sure that you must have.'

'So, tell me – I don't need the salad dressing. Fuck that.'

Khalil presses his forefinger against his lips, signalling Jimmy to quieten.

'I ask what she means and she says I'm to take the Mac Kenzie Road, it's called this by the Fijian soldiers, a dirt road that runs for about fifteen kilometres in a loop between orange groves, tobacco plantations and stands of pine, ideal places to launch Katyusha rockets towards some SLA positions. Drive up the road to Brahim Sourb's deserted place and you'll see, she said.

She knew I wouldn't have gone there by myself and so she told her youngest boy to show me. Bring him home safely, Khalil Abbas, she said. She had bad eyes that woman, the eyes of a shark, cold and unblinking. I knew Sourb's place of old, but I said nothing.

She didn't like me for the way I lived under Israeli rule. I was a prostitute in her eyes, the worst kind, me and some of the others – she believed that we had prostituted our souls more than our bodies.

The child was no more than ten. He was keen to travel with me, the way children are for adventures. On the journey I asked how come he had been left behind in the initial rush to this place and he said his sister kept him home, but his mother had scolded her for doing it.

Allah was good – he was meant to go, and that was why I had been sent.

The pick-up's headlights bobbed along the road, a road broken by shellfire and neglect, through a canopy of trees, crashing gears as I descended to a Fijian checkpoint. The place was manned but the soldiers had no real interest in us – one ran his eye over the bed of the truck and asked our destination. The kid said Al Taki, a small nest of houses on the Mac Kenzie loop, and the soldier said he knew old Brahim Senior who used to live there and to pass on his regards. Must be a party on, he said. I wonder sometimes had they not been told of the kidnappings? Surely, they must have been. But it appears not – not until it was pointless them being told anything.

The night was warm and balmy, quiet.

The boy didn't have to tell me we had arrived – I saw the cars parked either side of a wide entrance, and more outside the derelict house. A grey house with ivy and black streaks of soot climbing its façade.

The house. It belonged to the Sourbs who moved out years ago to live in Sidon. I remember when wooden gates met you at the entrance and the avenue had a sweep of gravel that ended at steps leading to the veranda. The storm shutters were a sky blue and the windows were always clean and shining. Flowers and shrubs and a small fountain with lilies on top and frogs that croaked the night long were over-grown with weeds. A large rock formation stood next to the house and the Sourbs had cut into this, making a doorway and a cave. They had a wooden stairs leading to it – apparently the old man used to make his own wine and arrack and this was his base.

Shouting.

A lot of shouting, Sergeant.

It drew us around the back, through some pine to a clearing where a cedar tree stood strong of limb and scarred. The last of a small wood of them. This one, too, diseased and in the early stages of decay. Its bark, like the façade of the house, streaked with burning caused by exploding shells.

The American was dead.

He swayed on the tree, was poked at with sticks and taunted. His name was Blissett. In the noose beside him, about an arm's length away was your father – he was alive and kicking his legs out. Not death throe kicks but loud kicks, lashing out at the injustice of this act.

And no one said anything. And no one did anything. We watched the last kicks give out to a gentle swaying, ropes creaking. The small boy left my side, ran to your father. I thought he had his mother in him and wanted to spit and curse at swaying bodies but he grabbed your father's legs and tried to lift and he was crying and saying that this man was good, a good man, not American.

Of course, the men knew he was Irish.

But the blood lust for revenge had been too strong to allow for the difference, and in the birth rush of fresh guilt they cut him down, but . . .'

'Tell me.'

'The harm was done.'

'You kept this a secret all this time – you're not a murderer, took no part—'

'No part? I could have saved your father, stopped him from—'

Khalil cut himself short, gesturing with a sweep of his hand as though it were an axe.

A loose tongue is like a swollen river that has burst its banks – it has no control over itself.

'This place – can you bring me there?'

Khalil nods.

'The boy?'

'Your father used to be the Humanitarian Officer's

driver – he would often bring food and medicine supplies to the villages – that is how the boy recognized him.'

'So they took him away – left the American there.'

'Yes. The American swayed there, his khaki uniform blood and spittle stained, his features black and blue. He was, I like to think, half unconscious before they put the noose around his neck. Foolish, arrogant man travelling about Lebanon with the flag of the United States on his shoulder.'

'Do you know where they hid my father's body?'

Khalil lifts his chin.

This is it.

Lie, Khalil, lie.

'I don't know.'

'You must.'

'I don't – I have a vague idea, that's all, no more. A notion of several places.'

'Where?'

'I will take you – then, will you be satisfied?'

'No. Only when I have my father's remains will I be satisfied.'

'And if this is not possible?'

'It will be – I'm sure of it, Khalil.'

'They both received very bad hidings.'

'And?'

'Teeth knocked out, ribs broken, ears and noses hanging off.'

'Why were they attacked?'

'Why? To drive through a village in mourning for its dead – the main ally of their sworn enemy! Ah, Sergeant, come now.'

The Sergeant nods.

Khalil suggests that they get sleep. He has a spare mattress under a table in the shop.

'Bring it in here. There is spare linen in a chest and a pillow. Air them by the heater for some minutes before you retire.'

'In the morning, Khalil?'

'Yes, in the morning, if Allah spares me, I will show you.'

15

The vomit he spews is worse than anything he has ever spewed – it smells foul, a bile the colour of rust with the fluidity of congealing blood. The pain in his lungs and ribs so severe that he bites on his duvet to stop from crying out. The pills he swallows are slow to kick in and don't until the sun begins to show its face above the northern hill, a mound shaped like a woman's breast with a teat of spindly pine.

A pain so bad that he doesn't care if his life ends at this precise moment, if he is never to haggle over another dollar with another soul, if his shop is to close and the tin walls and roof to fall in, if the man staring at him with a concerned and questioning look ever comes to understand that some things are best left alone, that it is sometimes unwise to disturb the dust of the past.

'Are you O.K.?' Jimmy says.

He is a picture framed by the doorway, looking out at Khalil, the unkempt yard.

O.K.? He has been asked some stupid questions in his time, but this, dear Allah, is the worst. The sickness has turned its coat inside out. Has he no eyes to see?

'I'm fine.'

The Irishman moves into the yard, lights up a pair of cigarettes and proffers one to Khalil who nods his appreciation before he sucks in the smoke and shuffles, his torso leaning forward, to a plastic chair pulled from another by Jimmy. He sits and massages his side – perspiration caused by pain drying to salt on his forehead.

He had vomited in his bed, on himself and the floor, the smell rancid. Vomited again in bushes, on roses.

Squeezed as dry as a tyre-squashed lemon, reduced to a dry retching and finally a dull throbbing pain. Grateful that the flood tide of his misery has receded. Drained, he feels drained. Rattled.

'Do you want coffee?' Jimmy asks.

'Turkish, you can make Turkish?'

'No.'

'Maxwell then – it's in the cupboard. I must show you how to make Turkish coffee, but another time. It appears you might be a slow student – given you can't see death shadowing a man's face.'

He drinks two cups of coffee, but it tastes like nothing as

the bile has put too much of a coating on his tongue.

'Yes – you do look a very sick man.'

'Yes. Dying. Last night was the worst yet.' He taps his ribs and then his chest, 'The poison spreads.'

'Cancer?'

Nods, 'Heart, too – the body is breaking down.'

'I'm sorry.'

Khalil waves a hand, 'It comes to us all.'

'Yes, it does – in ways many of us would not expect.'

'Yes – I don't think, Sergeant, that I am up to travelling today – perhaps tomorrow.'

O'Driscoll is subdued. Khalil senses his frustration.

'Tomorrow,' O'Driscoll says with dejection, sounding as though the day was far off.

'I hope, yes. My illness is a nuisance to both of us.'

'I can't afford too many delays.'

'A day or two late in starting will not matter – Lebanon is not such a big country. And I have only a small number of places to show you – where your father might be buried. We can wait a day or two, until I am strong enough to see the journey through.'

With more than some reluctance O'Driscoll says, 'O.K., the day after tomorrow, Monday – it'll give me time to arrange a Land Cruiser.'

Khalil sighs, 'Good. Good. You realize that after fifteen years my memory might not be reliable?'

'I will search where you show me.'

'And that one of these places was bombed by the Israelis.'

'I—'

'You might see many bones and skulls where I take you, unearthed by the bombs.'

'I know what I'm looking for – I've dental charts, photographs – I know what he wore at the time.'

'Good, that will be a help. At least you have a needle in the haystack.'

'My mother gave him a gold Claddagh ring for his birthday – two hands holding a heart, if the heart—'

'Faces the knuckles it means that the heart is spoken for – I know, I have seen many Irish with this ring in my shop.'

'Her initials, MO'D, are on the inside of the band. He had a silver capped front tooth – a tooth he broke during his soccer days – see, Khalil, I will easily identify my father – that is if these items weren't stolen.'

'Monday, then.'

Jimmy pauses as he makes to enter the shop with the mattress he has rolled up, ignoring Khalil when he says he will tidy it away.

'Are you afraid of dogs, Khalil?'

'Are we talking about canines or a certain breed of woman?'

'Canine,' smirks Jimmy.

'No.'

'Excellent – I have a dog coming with me – all the way from Ireland. Jake, he's an Alsatian.'

'I see,' Khalil says, wondering at what use he has in mind for the animal, 'and what—'

'He smells for the dead.'

When O'Driscoll leaves for MP Coy, Khalil puts his soiled sheets and duvet in a black bag for dumping, washes the floor, then himself, sprays the room with cedar deodorizer. Waters his vomit from the roses before the sun gets at them.

'Smells for the dead – indeed! His nostrils will seize if he breathes in all of Lebanon's missing dead.'

Khalil sleeps in his wife's bed. Dr Frere had come and gone, prescribing stronger medicine and bed rest. Zarifa and Adeeba had not long departed for Saad Tours in Sidon to book Adeeba's flight to London. It had been agreed – her aunt couldn't wait to see her. Daoud went with them, leaving Dahab to stay and keep an eye on the patient.

They made a joke of this, calling him a patient, as if the notion of him being one was ludicrous. A child feigning illness to seek attention.

He has lost weight.

Frere had touched his shoulder before he left, a touch telling him to hang on in there.

'You will give me something to kill the pain when I ask?' Khalil said.

'Yes.'

'You know what I mean – let us be clear?'

'It is something I'm asked for too often, Khalil – I hope it will be done for me when my time comes, inshallah,' he tapped his breast.

Dahab had dropped in once to see how he was, left him a tray with tea and some rice cakes.

The TV is on, its picture alive, the sound low. All he wants is the presence of a voice and a moving screen – better distractions than the radio.

Feels better, not much better, but a little.

In a few minutes he will get to his feet and sit outside on the balcony, taste some cranberry juice. Using field binoculars he will watch the sea and Mingi Street, the daily routine of the soldiers and civilian workers in the 2 km long Unifil compound.

He likes these small intrusions into others' lives. A habit that has its origins during a time when he took his siestas in the house. Occasionally, thieves came from the mountain villages and acted like carrion crows if they saw an unattended building.

Though there was a neighbourhood watch scheme most people stayed indoors during the burning midday sun – twice Khalil's shop had been raided and stock taken. In sixteen years' trading he supposes that it is not a bad innings.

He will read the *Daily Star*, a revamped newspaper

published in Beirut that Jesso gets in from the capital, courtesy of the Italian pilots who fly the UN helicopters twice daily to and from the capital.

White doves – noisy beasts. Whirring blades are shadows of knives across the inshore waters – always the choppers travel over the sea to Beirut, the detour the safest option during the war years when UN helicopters were shot at and sometimes downed.

In a few minutes, yes, get up – for now just be content to rest and think.

He had discussed things with Zarifa, telling her where his money was held and that the account was in both of their names. She will have enough to live on if she is careful. He knows some widows who have no choice but to eat like birds – she can eat a little more.

She told him of the harsh words exchanged between herself and Adeeba this morning.

About Ossie. Always Ossie.

Zarifa had said something derogatory about him and Adeeba flared up. A volcano spitting lava. Zarifa said nothing in response – had simply felt the waters to test her suspicions – Adeeba and Ossie and whoever and whoever else after that – a pair, a trio, a quartet, eventually.

Ah, Adeeba, if only I could make you wise, give you clear eyes.

A robin lands on the sill.

Come in, small visitor. Aren't you lucky that Cutie isn't here?

Sunlight burnishes its red breast. Beak twitches, eyes dart – flies away.

He eases from bed, head a little groggy, his stomach empty, bladder full. After showering he dresses in beige cotton slacks, check T-shirt and new sandals, cushion soles, Velcro straps. Douses his cheeks in Brut aftershave and combs his hair through with oil.

The retired businessman. Ailing.

A grand closing down sale.

Doors shut for the final time.

Goodbye to the Street.

The wedding – Kasni had dropped in with the invitation. His sister is marrying a French soldier. It will be a great day. Zarifa declined to let him upstairs when he asked to see Khalil, said he was asleep, that he had a bad night.

Khalil heard her saying this.

'Why didn't you let him up to see me?' he asked when she visited his room.

'He only wanted to see how dead you were.'

'How dead I was, woman – I could have spoken with him about Dahab and Daoud – asked him to deal with Aziz.'

'And you know he would have told you to keep out of it.'

'No.'

'Yes, Khalil, why do you think he called? He could have had

someone else drop the card over – obviously Aziz wanted to talk to you through him.'

'What's to become of them?' he asked.

'She is good company and the boy is well-behaved.'

'Yes.'

'But they can't stay here, Khalil, not for too long more – these arrangements never work out.'

He nodded.

'Dahab is young enough to attract other men. She will find someone else and then he will move in with her.'

Khalil knew where she was leading but didn't guide her.

'There is talk of her having men.'

'Having men?'

'Unifil soldiers.'

'Yes, she does their washing and ironing.'

'Don't pretend to be stupid!'

He smiles, 'I don't have to pretend.'

Eliciting no response from Zarifa he continues, 'Ah, she is friendly with a couple of them.'

'She is a selective prostitute.'

'Zarifa!'

'It's true – she gives certain men her favours.'

'Zar—'

'She told me herself.'

'A woman needs to be loved.'

'Just so you know, Khalil, where Aziz is coming from.'

'I know where he is coming from – and I thought you did, too.'

His mild rebuke startles her. Her lips tighten, revealing thick vertical lines above her upper lip.

'Perhaps, you hold more affection for her than you do for the boy.'

'There are affections and affections, Zarifa – what I feel for you runs deeper.'

The lines disappear, replaced by a certain look of satisfaction. Ah, she buries the truth of his condition, knows but has not accepted – jealousy – Dahab? Absurd.

He has not forgotten the role she played in her older boy's death. Her ambition, her lies ruined him. Zarifa was right – who knew what ambitions remained locked in Dahab's heart.

Had she learned her lesson?

Would history repeat itself with Daoud?

Allah – breathe against the boy's back and push him to safety.

He pads to the balcony and sits on an easy chair, his newspaper and juice waiting for him. The pain is dull and throbbing, like threatening cloud on the horizon, waiting for a favourable wind to push it inshore.

So near to death and still so much worry.

Zarifa – she has inner strength. Still, she will be a woman alone in the world, with no one to turn to, except other widows – and the war has left enough of those around – so not a major worry, not Zarifa. Never was – typical of her. Strong, reliable, keeper of his secret, wears it like she had never been told anything.

Adeeba – what can he do about her? She has so much of his mother in her. That air of self destruction she is blind to.

Daoud – the son he always wanted, his employee – growing up in two war zones – one waged outside and another waged behind his door. He needs to be free of both.

O'Driscoll – searching for his father's remains.

He doesn't need to see such a sight, in spite of the worm inside him.

I am not sure that it is the right thing to do, to lead him on a false expedition.

But I have made the decision.

Have you, Khalil?

Yes, Voice.

Yes – moral cowardice again. Then it's a family trait.

I'm no coward.

No? Dr Frere – please kill me when the pain gets too much.

I make no apologies for that.

You owe O'Driscoll his father.

No. I owe the father, not the son. I can't give the man back to his son. No.

You'll die in agony, Khalil.

Go!

Khalil gets to his feet and puts his hands on the stone parapet. A slight breeze cools his forehead. He shuts his eyes. Opens them. Sees his Mercedes coming up the road, approaching the house. Turning about he decides he is well enough to greet them.

Why not give them a treat, even if it is a false dawn?

Dahab lets them in. Daoud first, then Adeeba – a scowling Adeeba who manages a smile for him. Zarifa next, her hands on her temples and looking at Adeeba's disappearing back.

'She won't go. I stood there, Khalil, ordering the ticket when she says, "I'm not going." Can you imagine?'

'Adeeba!' he says.

She shows her head round the kitchen door, 'Papa?'

'Why?'

'I'm meeting Ossie – we are coming to an arrangement.'

'What sort of arrangement – you can mind his other wife's children?'

'No, my own.'

He and Zarifa exchange glances.

How can this be? She can't have children. She has told us this so often.

'Before we split up I had been attending a gynaecologist – you need to hear the details?'

From the kitchen Dahab says, 'The tea is ready.'

Cutie meows.

Daoud asks if he can count stock tomorrow.

He likes to add.

Zarifa brushes past Adeeba.

He stares at his daughter. Tears in his eyes. And in hers.

'You don't understand, Adeeba, because I've never told you.'

'Understand what?'

'Nothing, nothing – it's too late, too late.'

'Papa?'

'No – congratulations.'

Part II

16

Early morning traffic is light on the street. A couple of cars murmur towards the coastal road, a pair of youths pitch their voices above their whining scooter, dirty tongue of smoke trailing from its exhaust. A tractor's bones clang and rattle along the asphalt.

Showing his ID card to a tired looking sentry, Jimmy O'Driscoll passes through the French Wadi Gate carrying fresh pitta bread and squeezed orange juice he had bought some minutes before from a stubbled vendor. His MP brassard saves queries from the sentry about curfew hours.

In Italair, a chopper's blades are starting to mount towards a crescendo. Kicking up a breeze, blowing dust his way. He hurries by the wire perimeter fence, shielding his eyes against the grit storm and takes a left at a T-junction, onto the camp's main road. To his right lies the Polish hospital, the Fire

Brigade, the prefabricated living quarters of the Polish medical units, the scrapyard, the tall tower from which a French sentry monitors sea traffic. To his left, a short way and then left again, climbs a steep hill leading to the International Officers' Mess, the different houses belonging to the contingents serving in Lebanon, offices, the old customs post, headquarters of the OGL, Observer Group Lebanon, the main dining mess, the civilian admin block and the library. The cenotaph etched with the names of Unifil's fallen, complete with apron of shorn green grass, sprinklers and ribbon of red pathway. Days ago he saw that the leaves on the wreath he placed at its base had been burned yellow by the sun, the ink faded on the small card he folded between the arms of leaves. Cut into black marble stone his father's name in gilded letters.

Farther along the main road, there are the log groups, the vehicle maintenance and repair yards, the PXs, Post Exchanges, the Rubb Hall and gym. To his right lies MP Coy, crossed flintlocks etched on the duty room's gable wall, its parade square cum volleyball court, a mini barracks of its own, Camp Martin, called after an MP who died while serving with the unit in the early 1980s.

The roll call is ongoing, the Sergeant Major breathing names as though each is a disease one should pray not to contract.

Pauses for a second or two after airing a name which he appears to hold in particular disdain.

'Where is Sergeant Vulurula?' he booms. Rigid back, blue beret perched on his head like something he was born with.

Silence.

'Ah, here he is – Sergeant Vulurula, parade is at o seven thirty hours and not o seven thirty-two fucking hours!'

'Sorry, Sir.'

'You're always fucking sorry. No excuses, fall in.'

The Major waits until Vulurula joins the parade before saying, 'Parade, attention!'

Heels snap together, a couple of pairs out of synchronization – the professional civilian police in their own countries.

'Dismiss! Report to your places of employment.'

Heels part – the usual out of sync.

Jimmy on his way into the Mess had taken the route behind a row of parked jeeps.

Last thing he needs is to have Tom crowing into his ear about missing Parade, although technically speaking he isn't attached to MP Coy – he's a lone ranger, given a month to investigate this case. A lend of a dog and a lend of time. Answerable only to the Chief of Staff at home.

He helps himself to a mug from a tray of them on the margin of the bar counter and makes for the Burco boiler. Remnants of coffee at the base of its tin are rock hard, the colour of mountains he had seen in Northern Iraq. He chips away a chunk and drops it into the mug, adds water and Israeli long life milk. His orange juice and pitta bread he keeps for lunch as the midday meal in the International Mess isn't worth the walk up the hill and the wait in the queue.

Jimmy passes through into a veranda with a bamboo roof, the sea a yawning expanse of blue before him, the waves quiet. Sits in an easy chair, its cushion well fluffed, showing the wear of too many arses.

Since the old man had opened up about the night, Jimmy had been going over his words, a card player trying to read all the cards Khalil had and hadn't shown. The old man, crafty as Sin, would seldom be guilty of saying the wrong thing.

Jimmy closes his eyes. Think! Focus!

The scent of the sea is strong – salt and sun-kissed water and rocks.

Focus.

Let's talk about light, shall we?

Evening time; hangings by torch and car light – how close was Khalil standing to the ropes – the depth of a grave away, its width?

Nearer?

If he had a clear view then he must have been pretty near. But you'd see people hanging from a distance. I mean for fuck's sake, they were hung from the limb of a tree.

He saw the Clint Eastwood movie, *Hang 'em High,* on BBC1 about three nights before flying to the Leb, and wondered if he were being told something from beyond. He has a garble of loose thoughts in his head concerning religion, afterlife and everything else incapable of giving a straight fucking earthbound answer.

What happened later?

Does Khalil really know where they buried my father? Was he present or did someone tell him? A few places? Had his father's body been moved to another grave because Borge was closing in? Or for some other reason? Did Khalil turn the earth with a shovel and pat it down? Yeah. Present all right – had to be. He's worried about his memory failing him, that he might arrive at the wrong location and he knew of the air strikes disturbing the graves. His tongue had too easy a familiarity with places he claimed never to have visited.

Questions.

Khalil needs a good grilling. Patience, though, a little patience for the moment must be right. Yet not too much patience because the old man's health is failing. Khalil is the last living witness to his father's death. A roll call of those gone before him.

Push him too much and he might clam up or use his illness as an excuse not to travel.

Jimmy half expects this to happen.

So many other witnesses have placed Khalil at the scene. And there were witnesses who stated that three men took down his father and put him into a car boot – Khalil, Brahim Sourb and Jesso's father. That puts Khalil bang in the centre of things.

Can't breathe that to him, though. Yet. The last investigator ran into a brick wall when he tried – Khalil refused to speak with him, about anything.

Don't dwell on his lies. Press him for the truth – when the time is right.

Khalil comes across as a decent man. His own experiences and those of others have hewn him a countenance of wisdom. He is a person whom you would respect without cause, a giver of sound advice.

He is a walking nest of lies and half truths.

He'll reassure him that there will be no repercussions, no revenge, legal or otherwise, attempted against his family, their names spared from the media. These things are obviously of some importance to him, why else would he harbour the whereabouts of his father's remains? Khalil isn't a bad man and only a bad man would do such a thing.

Jimmy smells the man's sickness, even now, hours later, it clings to his nostrils, his clothes.

Opens his eyes when he hears a Fijian talk in his mother tongue. The pair start for a table farthest away, one carrying a Bible the other a long face. Vulurula.

Tom Hennessy, the Major, prefers the senior NCOs from the respective contributing nationalities to discipline their junior MPs. Blighting a man's conduct sheet is something he is loath to do – the last resort.

Tom shows, following his sigh. Removes his blue beret, its band leaving a red impression on his forehead.

'Your bloody dog was barking the whole night long, Jimmy, honest to Jaesus, where did you get him? Whining and barking – he almost did my head in.'

'He must have made strange with someone passing by.'

'Bollocks, he wanted to get his hole off the drug dog, that's what – fucking Norwegians in bitching this morning, honest to Jaesus – they love to whinge – complaining about Jake upsetting Heidi their drug dog. I've a good mind to let Jake in to do the business and give them a load of fucking mongrels to cry about.'

The Major's about fifty, lean and fit and with dark curly hair turning silvery. He likes to garden and build patios, doesn't drink – used to but quit, sometimes confides that he is still quitting.

'So, tell me, did you learn anything new from that oul fella?'

'He's going to bring me to a few places.'

'The report gives you some clues as to the—'

'Locations that were searched – the investigators hadn't got the benefit of an eyewitness showing them the sites.'

'I hear he's dying.'

'He is.'

'Is he being level with you?'

'No.'

'What are you going to do about that?'

'What can I do? Nothing. He's the best shot I've got.'

Tom glances at his watch. Frowns. Says that it's time he got back to the office. He's to sort out the detachment allowance, have it ready for the Dogface, Detachment Commander's, meeting tomorrow or else there'll be grumbles and tears.

'If I can help in any way, Jimmy, let us know.'

'A car?'

'Sure.'

'For a week?'

'Fine – do you need a volunteer to travel with you – someone to take care of Jake?'

'That'd be a great bonus – anyone in mind?'

'Me.'

'Fine.'

Tom knew his father, joined up at the same time and trained together as recruits. They spent long evenings on kitchen duties as they waited for their platoon to reach its training strength. Tom won the Best Soldier Award, while Dad collected the Best Shot Award at their passing out ceremony. Old photographs of men in uniform, taken indoors because of adverse weather conditions, all smiles after completion of gruelling weeks of training – a handful of them dead, culled by accident and disease and a murder.

'Great – it'll get me away from the fucking lot of them. Arseholes.'

Jimmy smiles.

'Nothing only little Mafias in here.'

Tom goes on to talk about the Poles caught smuggling car radios across the border, and how, the next day, when they were being repatriated the Yids found packets of cigarettes taped to their bodies – these fucking Poles don't give up. About the Nepalese cooking mussels in their billet and the Ghanaians skinning a dead cat and eating it on the beach. The Fijians cutting a pig's throat, the squeals of the animal.

Fuck, such a place.

'Want to hear a good one, Jimmy? I held a room inspection the other day – just to keep the manky fuckers on their toes – the CO came with me, but he's fucking blind – there could be shit under his nose and he wouldn't see or smell it – this Norwegian fella had a fucking pet lizard in his room – he wasn't in his room, of course, fucker deliberately forgot that he had to hand over his room – so, I went looking for him to get rid of the fucking thing. Big green yoke it was, in a glass case, an iguana or something.

'I met Haverson and asked him about his buddy, that I wanted to speak with him about his lovely lizard. Your man says, "Do you like him, Sir? I've got one the exact same. His name is Julius and Pers calls his Caesar." Manky fuckers, the lot of them, Jimmy.

'Pain in my hole, Jimmy. No one wants to do anything any more – the Norwegians complain about the Irish holding all the key appointments, the Ghanaians and the Nepalese spend their nights watching porn movies, the Poles guzzle vodka and smuggle and the Irish are pissed off with the Finns – you know our crowd, it takes fucking nineteen to twenty years to make sergeant from corporal, that's if you've an excellent record, and the Finns are here a week and they've gone from being useless corporals to useless fucking lieutenants. In a week, I ask you – imagine – their Minister of Defence must be God to get things done in seven days. I'll be glad to get out of here for a while, before I go mental.'

'Tell me, Tom, how does a xenophobic end up in charge of foreign troops?'

'That's the army for you.'

Jimmy likes the Major if not his attitude. He's rough and ready, a man's man, a species caught between new and old worlds – someone who hasn't moved with the times. A widower who spends his time volunteering for overseas missions. Says he should qualify for Lebanese citizenship because he's punched in that much time here.

Jimmy makes his excuses to leave – plans to check on Jake and then get his head down for a couple of hours. It'll be great to have another driver on board. Instead of minding the road he can watch out for subtle changes of mood in

Khalil's features, the shadow of the sun must cross the rock face at some time.

Tom says, 'Let's hope we hit the jackpot – and I know that oul fucker, Khalil, he sold me a gammy radio the trip before last. He won't pull the wool over my eyes again.'

'Your CO won't mind you taking the time off?'

'He'll be glad to see the back of me.'

Jimmy imagines that must be so and smiles.

Jake is kennelled in an air-conditioned oxide painted shed – divided by a sheet of chipboard. Heidi has him driven wild with lust. But she's heading back to her dog platoon in Norbatt this evening, so he might settle in himself.

Jimmy feeds Jake and rakes a comb through his fur, promises him a walk later, when it's dark and the air is cooler. Jake is three years old and lives at home with Jimmy, has two cats and an old terrier for company. Jimmy and Jake – sounds like a TV cop show. Jimmy has an army number and so has Jake – part of the newly established dog section formed last year to contend with the army's rising drug problem, and to aid the civil police. Jake's training in England an altogether new departure – searching for dead bodies – lost, long dead or a short while dead.

No proven success in Ireland yet, except for a body found in the Bog of Allen, a poor soul who committed suicide in the nineteenth century and by church law could not be buried in a consecrated grave. Grey shawl, leather shoes, buckles, and bones showing through bog-preserved flesh. Jake's success, a chance success.

Jimmy retires to his billet and draws his curtains against the day, sets the floor fan going, keeping it at low speed. Pops a beer from the fridge and sits on the edge of his bunk. Wrecked. Feels wrecked.

Slugs beer and turns on the radio. BBC World Service and *Sixty Seconds Around the World*. Undresses to his boxers and slips in under the mosquito netting, lies on top of the clean sheet and closes his eyes – searching for sleep.

Always searching. For sleep.

His father.

St Anthony, patron saint of things lost, help me.

St Jude, patron saint of hopeless causes, help me.

Is there anyone listening?

Sleep evades him. He grabs another beer and moves outside to sit under a parasol by a fence of meshed wire with knee-high weeds. He smells the sea, quiet tonight, and hears the drone of the Israeli patrol boats offshore. He turns his head to check a sudden movement in the corner of his eye. A cat. Good. Not a snake or a rat. He should be at home with Jo and his son, Barry, winding down on leave from the army, not here in Lebanon chasing his father's grave. Would be. If the likes of Khalil and his sort weren't murdering bastards.

17

Sunday morning, a smell of roasting chicken, the sun weak, the skies watery, the slightest of breezes blowing inland, rustling the leaves of the eucalyptus and orange trees in his neighbour's garden. A man who sits in Khiam Prison for killing his wife.

A quiet fellow, studious – a row – a knife pulled from a wooden block of them – a moment of madness. It happened during the khamsin, hot desert winds capable of soughing screws from the hinges of a man's mind. Last autumn Khalil gathered the oranges from the garden, unable to stand the sight and smell of decaying fruit.

Lazy day, Sunday – always that. Slow the world to a crawl on that day – bit of a Christian about him.

Khalil sits in his garden, smoking and drinking coffee. The boy plays with his kitten, and sometimes breaks off to dribble a ball about, panting to himself – 'Ryan Giggs, Ryan Giggs, goal!'

Adeeba spent last night in the shop. She did herself and Zarifa a favour because the tension between the pair was palpable. He had tried to soothe Zarifa's anger, telling her that Adeeba was a grown woman, that they could only counsel her – she had to make up her own mind.

'You didn't leave Dahab to fall on her own blade, did you?'

'There's a difference, Zarifa – a child is involved and trouble comes to Dahab – she isn't marching towards it, to embrace it – is she?'

'No – that girl of ours is stupid – probably gets it from your side of the family. Not mine – stupid, crazy girl.'

'Don't say that, Zarifa – don't ever say that!'

Zarifa straightened herself up to look down at him. She had forgotten. His mother, of whom he thought she knew nothing.

'Sorry, Khalil – but it's upsetting to see her— '

'I know. But she loves him.'

'Loves – it's a stupid love. He can do whatever he likes to her and still she goes back to him.'

'We can't stand in her way – there's a baby to think of, and you must be there for her. We must fend for our own – even if we think they are undeserving of such fending.'

'Do you believe she's pregnant?'

'Yes.'

'I don't.'

'No? You think it's a scheme.'

'A scheme. Just to give her a reasonable excuse for going back to him. Yes.'

'Zarifa – listen, all you can do is to be here for her.'

Zarifa said nothing, slapped her hands on her knees and sighed. Her legs ached and she was due to have the operation on the veins next week. She told him this quietly, her words faint as though she didn't like complaining in the face of his illness.

'I'll be away for two or three days,' he said, 'But I'll be back before you go in. Perhaps I will admit myself into Saint George's, yes? Let them promise me all sorts of things, keep me hoping until they've bled me of money – we might get beds next to each other.'

She nods, frowns – she knows him so well. He sometimes forgets how well. The little ruse of cracking a joke a poor effort at disguising his other news. He's not the fog he likes to think he is.

'Where are you going and why has that Irish MP been—'

'The hangings.'

Clouded features give way to sudden realization, 'Oh. And?'

'He is looking for his father's body.'

'Khalil!'

'I know. Old sins cast long shadows.'

'What do you intend to do?'

'Show him a grave, a couple of graves – what else can I do?'

'Tell him the truth.'

'No!'

Silence.

'I can't do that, Zarifa.'

'It has been left for you to do.'

'No.'

'You must. You have to.'

'Leave me alone.'

'Khalil . . .'

'No, Zarifa, I will not discuss this with you.'

'You should!'—

'Yes, I know, I know.'

'Show the son what became of his father.'

'No. I will show him graves – in Tyre, in Beirut – I will show him fields of bones and then apartment blocks – and I will look at them and tell him that his father rests there.'

'You are like Adeeba – you will do whatever you want. Right or wrong you will still do it. This is an opportunity to purge yourself of the guilt that's been haunting you.'

'It is too late for that – always has been.'

'No. You haven't the courage, Khalil.'

'Courage? Woman, listen to me, it would be cowardly of

me to divulge everything – I have taken away his father from him. Should I now replace his living memory of his father with the memory I could give him? Should I do that, Zarifa – tell me?'

'No.' Said without hesitation.

A silence lasting minutes and then she told him that the situation regarding Dahab and Daoud had resolved itself, and how it had come about. Dahab will talk to him.

Khalil pours fresh coffee.

His pain has subsided a little, but there's a nagging permanency about it now.

Wants to piss but can't piss – pisses when he no longer feels the urge to – embarrassing and bewildering. Summer and he wears the long robe he usually only dons during winter – over his slacks so the leaks when they happen don't show.

There's the smell, too – but he excuses himself from company and so the smell isn't a problem – he is gone before noses crinkle. They would only get the slightest taste of his smell and perhaps secretly blame each other before his absence assumed significance. They would sigh and nod – it is permissible for old men to smell their age. Is it not?

Dignity. The stripping of his greatly disturbs him.

He pours orange juice into fresh tumblers and calls the boy over.

'Khalil?'

A handsome boy, beautiful eyes, innocence.

'Sit, come sit down – we need to talk.'

The boy pulls out a chair. He has a light film of perspiration on his forehead, his face in need of a good wash. Khalil pushes the tumbler across, 'Drink a little – being Ryan Giggs is hard work.'

The boy swallows and settles his tumbler on the table.

'I'm closing the shop. For good.'

'I heard – Mamma said you might.'

'There'll be a closing down sale – tomorrow, I need you to take note of all stock, you and Adeeba – make notices – the sale will be next Thursday. Eh, no lazy day that day for any of us.'

Khalil strokes his chin, 'Now, your father and mother – let us talk man to man. O.K., Daoud?'

'O.K.'

'Do you want to live with Aziz?'

'No. I don't like his new wife.'

'I've spoken to your mother, Daoud.'

'Yes, Mamma said – I don't want to go to Canada. It's cold. I want to go to England.'

'Ah, yes – Manchester United – it's cold in England, too.'

'I like football, Khalil – I saw Lebanon playing Oman – it was great.'

'Your mother's brother is in Canada – you should go there – it is a lovely country.'

'You were there?'

'Yes. My biggest mistake was not staying.'

Liar Khalil.

Ah, it's for the good.

So – you lie to save pain. Is that it?

And for expediency, too.

At least you're honest.

I try to be.

Voice – I was only joking.

'Mamma says I'm being awkward, but I like it here with you and Zarifa.'

'I am old, Daoud, and Zarifa is getting old – we won't be here forever.'

'Papa says he will kill Mamma if she tries to leave Lebanon.'

'Then he isn't to know, Daoud.'

The child sits silently. Fidgets with the tumbler, eyes avoiding Khalil's.

'Daoud, you mustn't tell him.'

Daoud nods.

Khalil intends to give most of the money from the closing down sale to Dahab – it should cover her initial living expenses in Canada. She had come to him with the idea earlier that morning, when she had brought him his coffee – her brother had sent some money and with what she had saved she and Daoud could leave.

She doesn't need his money but it's for Daoud – he will insist she accepts it for Daoud's sake. They are flying out from Beirut International next Saturday morning. Would he drive them there? she asked.

Yes. Yes, he would. Certainly. See them off into a new life.

'Think about it, Daoud – think about going – the world is a small place – it's as easy to come back as it is to leave.'

'O.K., I'll think about it – can I go play ball?'

'Yes, of course.'

Another blood vessel pops on his forearm. He thinks how his arms have thinned to matchsticks – how could this happen when they were once so strong and thick with muscle and veins? Allah, a thousand deaths before the real one – it is easy to understand why some prefer the immediacy of a bullet. Not for me, though – for me it is the long goodbye – has to be for I don't want to leave.

Strawberry blood clouds on his flesh – he remembers the same marks on his father's arms and neck. He presses a wad of tissue paper against the miniature geyser and waits the bleeding out.

His coffee is cold, the cigarette ash in the ornate ashtray, a brass plate supported by the humps of three camels, holds his gaze. He chews on his lower lip and then breaking the spell he makes for the kitchen, feeding the bloodied tissue to a pedal bin.

'Something to eat, Khalil?' Dahab says.

Shakes his head. Can't speak for his stomach has climbed into his throat.

On his knees he leans his head over the toilet bowl – a western concept Zarifa insisted on installing in the house. He prefers to squat. You empty the bowels thoroughly and are less inclined to remain squatting than you would if seated comfortably – basking in the smell of your own shit.

Retches. And then, it flows.

He takes to the bed feeling as though it is his best friend.

He wakes late evening feeling refreshed. The pain and goose pimples have retreated.

Reaches out and thumbs the luminous switch on his lamp.

Someone has been in – a tray left on his bedside locker holds a plate of *fattoush,* a toasted bread salad with tomatoes, onions and mint leaves. Tempted, he picks at the mint leaves, chewing only, extracting the flavour.

Then, groggy and weak kneed he pads to the shower.

'You said nothing – just went to bed,' Zarifa scolds in the kitchen.

The tea on his lips, in his mouth, is a warm treasure he holds before swallowing. Rich, strong, sugary tea – it can't be beaten.

The portable TV is on, some American show – Jerry

Springer – what is it Dawson used to call him, the MP who told him what Mingi meant? Ah, yes, 'That gobshite.'

'Gobshite, Khalil?' Daoud says, looking up from his supper of cornflakes.

'Khalil!' Zarifa says.

'What does gobshite mean?' Daoud asks.

Khalil laughs, 'I can't say it in front of Zarifa.'

'Say it, Khalil.'

'No.'

'Is it a bad word?'

'Yes.'

'Like fuck, yes?'

Silence.

'Daoud! Stop that, wait until I tell your mother,' Zarifa says.

'Gobshite,' Daoud says.

Khalil mimes the alternative meaning behind Zarifa's back.

'Asshole,' Daoud says, laughing.

'Aunt Zarifa – that's what gobshite means – asshole.'

Though a little cross Zarifa can't prevent a smile breaking out.

It is good to have such young life in the house. The place will be very quiet without him, Khalil thinks.

'Dahab?' Khalil says, when the laughter has subsided.

'With Aziz – in his car out the front,' Zarifa says.

190

'Why didn't you tell me?'

'And have you interfere – again? – this time, Khalil, you will have to step over me to get out.'

His eyes light on Daoud. The worry of the boy. Allah, let her not be foolish enough to fall for his lies of a fresh start. Is she safe in the car with him? Is he with her?

Silence.

'Adeeba?'

'She's closing the shop, should be here in a few minutes.'

'Good, I need to discuss things with her, about tomorrow and Thursday's sale.'

'And with me, too,' Daoud says.

'Of course.' A pause then continues, whispering, 'I'm not a gobshite.'

'What's that, Khalil?' Zarifa says, pretending she hasn't heard.

'Nothing.'

The boy caps his mouth with his hand to stem laughter.

Khalil enjoys this little mischief making.

Daoud frowns, 'Cutie – I better go and get her.'

Zarifa says, 'It has not dawned on him that his kitten won't be travelling with him.'

'Don't tell him – not until we're at the airport.'

Dahab comes in a short while later, massaging her upper arm. Daoud is in bed.

Khalil shoots Zarifa a look of caution. Words can be stones falling on glass.

'Are you feeling better, Khalil?' Dahab says.

'A little, and how are things with you?'

She sighs and lowers herself to a chair, 'We went to Sami's grave. The sun is beautiful to watch – the way it falls from the sky into the sea.'

'It is.'

'He wants me to forgive him.'

'Yes.'

'I said I would – but it is a lie, Khalil, I want to go. I have to, for my sake, for Daoud's.'

'Well—'

'He will come here when he hears that I have gone – he will come looking for Daoud.'

'We will deal with that when the time comes.'

'You don't know what he is like in a temper.'

'I do. I have heard and seen the consequences.'

'And you're not afraid?'

'Not for myself, but for Zarifa and Adeeba.'

'I am sorry for bringing this trouble upon you.'

Khalil regards her with some amusement and tells her not to be silly – what are neighbours for?

He expects it but is nevertheless disappointed that Zarifa doesn't echo his sentiments.

Allah, watch over us. Give me the strength to see these

problems through. Not to leave Zarifa in danger, to spirit away Dahab and Daoud, to see Adeeba settle here with her baby, to leave the Irishman thinking he has done everything humanly possible to retrieve his father's remains.

18

In the bleak early hours of Monday, Khalil sips at his glass of tea – whisks the miniature spoon in the miniature glass, stirring its sweetness to life. Contemplates. He hates this sort of morning, being up and awake and alone at this hour – the dead hour. A ghost before his time – haunting a place when he should be in bed, asleep in his room or with Zarifa in hers after lovemaking. Or in his shop – a shop once so important to him, but which is lessening in its intensity of importance.

He checks a travel bag Zarifa packed for him last night – pills, a change of clothes, his old walking boots with the dust of his old energy on them, the tread worn to a shine – ah, but they used to be so comfortable – his camel leather wallet containing denominations of Lebanese pounds and American dollars, two bottles of spring water.

His burgundy coloured telephone and address book carries some names that no longer exist – uninhabited addresses punctured with bullet holes and in a lot of cases smashed by shells.

Khalil had told Adeeba to give O'Driscoll their home phone number. It isn't something he likes divulging as he prefers to keep home and work life separate, but O'Driscoll's business has a foot in each of Khalil's worlds.

He rang late last night to ask Khalil if the search was still on, if he felt up to travelling.

'I think so, I think I will be O.K.'

'Good – where and at what time will I collect you?'

Khalil gave him directions to his house, said to come early, before first light, adding that he would keep an eye out, not to beep the horn. Many people around here take more exception to a car horn sounding than to the muezzin commencing the first call to prayer. In Lebanon the car horn rests at night.

Cutie meows to draw his attention, interrupting his train of thought. Khalil drains his tea and tends to Daoud's pet, pouring long life milk into his plastic bowl, a kitten quickly becoming a cat.

'Now stop purring and drink up.'

Engine noise reaches his ears. Taking his bag he opens the front door. A Land Cruiser, two men, a dog in the rear luggage space. Engine throbbing.

Zarifa calls him from a few steps down the staircase, 'Khalil!'

He looks back, simultaneously closing over the door, 'Yes, Zarifa?'

'Don't forget your mobile.'

'I have it.'

She comes down the stairs, a hand on the banisters, conscious of her bad legs, wincing.

Close to him, now, smelling of talc, she touches his elbow and slides her hand to his shoulder, squeezes.

Even in their young days he was never overly affectionate towards her. He felt awkward.

He leans forward and kisses her lightly on the forehead, mops up the tear that falls from her eye with the tip of his forefinger, caresses her lips with his and then says, opening the door, 'See you in a couple of days, Zarifa – take care.'

'You, too, Khalil.'

Eases the door shut behind him.

O'Driscoll is out, opening the front passenger door for Khalil. He wears a green T-shirt and khaki shorts, sandals, dog tags.

Khalil takes a step backwards in himself – dog tags – as the father wore them his son now wears them. Same, same.

The heater is on low, enough to keep the chill of dawn at bay. On introduction by O'Driscoll he shakes the hand of a man in the back.

'Tom Hennessy here, how are you doing, Mister Abbas?'

'I am fine, thank you.'

Hennessy has a gruff voice, impatient, a strong handshake. 'I'm the CSM with MP Coy.'

'Ah, the Major.'

'Yes.'

'I sometimes hear the MPs talking about you in my shop.'

'All nice things I'm sure – shower of whores – they wouldn't be talking about me unless they had something bad to say.'

Khalil smiles, turns his head and faces the windscreen. O'Driscoll flicks the wash to life, runs the wipers over dead midges and draws away. Turns left, heading downhill towards the sleepy Mediterranean waters, Mingi Street and Unifil Headquarters.

Meeting a T-junction he veers right and steps on the gas a little as they leave behind the closed up shacks of failed businesses, which Khalil's is soon to join.

A radio station plays a seventies hit, 'You're a Lady'.

At the small fishing harbour outside Mingi Street they come to a South Lebanese Army post. Hennessy alights to open and close the swing gate after the cruiser passes through. A soldier sitting on a Sherman tank's turret looks sullenly at them, cradling an AK rifle on his lap, stroking the barrel. A grin loose on his face.

'Fucking wanker,' Hennessy says, 'that's what he is – he doesn't have to demonstrate.'

Inching over the speed ramps and swerving between the nail bars placed strategically on the ground, O'Driscoll says, 'Where to, Khalil?'

'I'll tell you in plenty of time, for now go straight.'

Hennessy says, 'This fucking dog of yours has farted again. For . . .'

'Khalil, you haven't met Jake – he's my sniffer dog.'

'I smell him.'

It is not worth your while bringing him, but I can't tell you that.

Hennessy says, 'You've no problem getting Jake back home after the trip?'

'No – he'll be quarantined for a couple of weeks and have some tests done, then he'll be back with me. You know the Department with money – it costs almost fifty grand to train a dog for this line of work, so they're going to get value out of him. But then he's going to a new trainer because I'm shaking off the uniform.'

'For that money it should be able to lower a fucking window before it farts.'

Going on Hennessy adds, 'The Norwegians bury their dogs here – they have a pet cemetery near their HQ in Ebel as Saqi. I was there a few years ago – they have patrol dogs, drug dogs, bomb dogs – busy place – they have these crosses on the ground, kind of touching if you're a fucking animal lover, but sort of sickish if you're in between like me. I like a dog, always had dogs for pets – first one the sheep farmers poisoned, the second one bit my mother on the arse, drawing blood – she had to be put down, the dog that is, Jimmy – I hate cats. Cats I fucking hate. Me and cats don't see whisker to whisker at all. Just don't.' Pauses then says, 'Like I was saying, you know, the Norwegians don't bring their dogs home.'

'Well, it probably makes sense – a dog gets old, can't smell, won't work.'

'It sounds as though you gentlemen are talking about me,' Khalil says.

Hennessy laughs. He has a loud laugh, with a burr to it. O'Driscoll smiles.

'Oh, you're some fucker, Khalil, a waster – do you remember the radio you sold me?'

Khalil looks behind. The movement hurts his neck.

'Go on, you don't need to look at me with those innocent eyes.'

'I have sold many radios.'

'Ah, Jaesus, you remember me surely – you wouldn't give me my money back.'

'There were many who looked for their money back.'

'No wonder you've a big house in the village.'

'Exactly. Cheap radios sold for expensive money – I made loads of money.'

'You can't keep up with you guys at all – ye have the crookery down to a fine art.

A fine fucking art. Mingi men and Mingi shops – licensed to con.'

Khalil lets the words fly over his head, 'Yes, an art.'

They drive about 6 km, the coastal road climbing and twisting, when they see Charlie Swing Gate, the last SLA checkpoint on the road to Beirut, looming before them. There are no queues, so they pass through speedily enough.

About 200 m from Charlie Swing Gate – a Unifil position that has seen its share of lives lost to bomb and bullet – they show their ID cards to the Fijian infantry soldiers on duty. One queries Khalil's presence and says he shouldn't be travelling in a UN car. Jimmy passes documents over.

'They're signed by the Force Provost Marshal,' Jimmy says.

Khalil can see that the soldier is unimpressed.

'I'm sorry, Sergeant, but—'

Hennessy steps from the car and says, 'He's with us – now, enough of this posturing shit – where's your officer?'

'He is resting off duty,' says the soldier.

'You've seen my ID card – I am now going to show you my MP Warrant Card – it gives me authority to kick ass – now, when you address me, you'll call me Sir, is that clear?'

'I—'

'I want to speak with your officer.'

'But—'

'No buts, ands or maybes – if he's not here in two seconds flat I'm ringing the Force Commander and you know what he's liable to say, don't you?'

The soldier glances at his companion who raises his shoulders. The Force Commander is Fijian and intolerant of misuse of a petty power. Khalil knows enough about bluffing to know that Hennessy isn't. He is a man who'd use a hammer to crack an egg.

'Soldier,' Hennessy squints at the cloth name tag sewn above the other's breast pocket, 'Monuku – Private Monuku – you've got one second left.'

'O.K., Sir, go on, go on – your papers are in order.'

'Who are you fucking telling, soldier? Can't you see the MP insignia on the bumper?

Are you an MP?'

'No.'

'No, what?'

'No, Sir.'

'Good man – now, carry on.'

Hennessy climbs into the car. Jimmy edges away.

'I fucking hate that – it's in black and white under his nose, he checked our ID cards, recorded our vehicle reg. the lot – intent on acting the bollocks with us, that's all. I fucking hate that sort of shit.'

'I think he knows that now,' Jimmy says.

'Fuck him.'

Khalil says, 'I hope you never adopt that approach with the Hezbollah.'

'That's a different story – these guys are soldiers, those other fuckers are murderers.'

A stand of pine next to the road is scarred – rusted and blackened from a car bomb explosion, the dip in the road indicating the detonation point.

'The Fijian MPs tell me that a bird hasn't sung here since the explosion four years ago – eight people died – five Fijians,' Jimmy says.

'I've heard it, too, about the birds,' Khalil says.

Every so often O'Driscoll increases the volume on the Motorola set, waiting for a break in radio traffic before transmitting a check call to the Duty NCO.

'Take the Burma road,' Khalil says, 'and then a right after the next Fijian post.

O.K.?'

Khalil wonders how the Irishman will react when he sees the place where they hanged his father and the American officer.

Is the house still standing or the cave beside it? What of the once proud cedar, dying back then? Has it been chopped for kindling or to make souvenirs? Roots lifted and burned?

The car is cool, air-conditioning on full blast, as they drive uphill through the Fijian checkpoint he had driven through fifteen years ago with the small boy who was eager to see avenged his father's and brothers' deaths. A canopy of trees accompanies this road for a long way, until it bends for Al Hinniyeh village where the MPs like to set up their speed traps. Sunlight filters through the trees and lands on the asphalt in varying sizes and shapes – scattered pools of light.

Khalil used to live not too far away from here. The groves he and his father worked still produce fruit, the roads they walked are in better condition but still the same roads. The hillscape has changed a little with the Israeli compounds and their high earthen embankments, but the men on the donkeys with their panniers of fruit, the women balancing baskets on their heads, the minarets, the poverty, his father's eyes would recognize these facets of his former life. There are times he misses the old man and times he sees him in a mirror.

They drive on, the road tighter and dustier than Khalil remembers. He says nothing when he gets the feeling that they have gone past the gateway to Sourb's place. Is just about to breathe his doubt when his eyes trip on the turn in.

How could he believe that he would ever forget?

The pillars had crumbled, plundered for their conical cappings. They pass through, the weeds tall and scrunching underneath, approaching a house that is devoid of doors and windows. A storm shutter lies awry, clinging to the wall – some of its slats missing.

'Snakes,' Hennessy says, 'be mindful of them – I was bitten by one of the bastards a couple of years ago – was washing my hands in the dark and got bitten. The fucking pain – I went to the RAP, taking about twenty-two steps more than I thought I'd be alive to walk and they pumped me full of antidote. Poxed I was – to be bitten so close to a medical aid post.'

Jimmy says nothing.

The engine dies. Silence. Broken by Jake's pawing at the rubber mat, knocking about his aluminium water dish.

Jimmy rubs the back of his hand against his lips, his eyes on the house.

Jimmy's eyes pan the length of the house, its dark recesses, the cave mouth, whispers, 'Lead the way, Khalil.'

Khalil steps out. To a man accustomed to the car's air-conditioning, the heat of the day weighs heavily, oppressively.

Hennessy opens decent cracks in all the windows and asks Jimmy for the keys to park the cruiser in a shadier spot.

Khalil massages his side as if to pacify his pain and then commences his walk, heading towards the gable end of the house, head lowered a little as though on a walk of penance, running his worry beads. Cicadas chirp all around, a flurry of bird wings.

They do come back, Khalil thinks. In time.

Hennessy is close behind them, following in the track they'd fashioned in the scrub grass. Jake barks to protest at being left behind.

This time in daylight hours Khalil sees more clearly the bric-a-brac of ordinary life discarded by the Sourbs – pots, a frying pan, a mesh grill, its ribs showing through the soil, broken chairs, rags.

He looks hard at the spot where the cedar tree used to stand.

A grubby location for people to die – a small rectangular garden – why had he always imagined it as being larger?

'Here, it happened here,' Khalil says, a little harder of tone than intended.

19

The air is still, perfumed with the scent of wild anemones that grow in bunches here and there. The skies a radiant blue, emptied of cloud but scarred by a jet's vapour trails.

Jimmy squats, touches the site where the tree stood, feels the dry clay, sieves it between his fingers, stops to turn part of a dead root over in his palm. Lets it fall and rubs his hands free of soil.

'I brought a wreath with me, Jimmy,' Hennessy says. Like his words are walking on glass. 'The boys in the MP Club, me, we all chipped in.'

He dips his hand into a black sack and sets the wreath beside Jimmy – a ring of flowers – gilded pomegranates, ivy leaves, a spray of roses.

'Khalil, let's leave Jimmy here for a few minutes.'

They return to the car. Hennessy lets the dog out, secures

the lead's loop around the hitch and clips the end to the dog's collar. Pours water from a container into the dish.

The attention off him for a few seconds Khalil pops three pills, downs them with a swig of still water. Sits in the car then, out of the midday sun – flies dance against the windscreen.

Jake slurps – slapping of tongue against water – for a time this action is the only noise.

Hennessy pisses against the pillar, hand on hip, the other on his member. Pissing for ages – full of piss.

'Grand shady spot, this,' Hennessy says, getting behind the wheel.

'Yes.'

Specks of urine about his fly.

'He'll probably say a few prayers,' Hennessy says.

'I think so, too, yes.'

'Awful fucking tragedy – what made youse do such a thing?'

'I saw – I didn't do anything.'

'You stood by and watched innocent men being hanged.'

'I was there for one hanging – almost too late for that.' Raises his eyebrows and points them in Jimmy's direction, 'His father.'

'I hope the fuck, Khalil, you aren't stringing him along on some wild fucking goose chase. He needs to do this, he needs to bring his father's body home.'

'I know.'

'No wild-goose chase.'

Khalil meets the other's eyes, 'Let me tell you a story, and you should know this story already – there were two Irish soldiers in an outpost that overlooked Madjil Silm wadi. One of the soldiers was found dead and the other has never been seen since. This happened years ago – the missing soldier – many theories have been suggested – he is supposed to have been captured by the PLO and killed in an Israeli air strike on a cave outside Sidon where many hundreds were killed – the cave was sealed off by the authorities and designated as a mass grave.'

'And you're telling me this, why?'

'Lebanese soil holds many unmarked graves – we might not find his father.'

'But, listen – you bury a body it stays there, right?'

Khalil thinks of Yusef, how his body didn't remain in its burial plot.

'You work on the assumption that I buried or helped to bury this man.'

'Didn't you?'

'No.'

'I thought you did. Jimmy—'

'Knows that I can take him to several places where down through the years I had heard his father was buried.'

'What a very convincing, convenient yarn you spin,

Mister – what is your second fucking name anyway?'

'Abbas. You have already called me by it. Is your memory bad?'

'As bad as fucking yours, Mister Abbas.' He points his finger at Khalil and then at Jimmy, who is getting to his feet, 'He might buy it, but I fucking don't – now, if you do know be straight, bring us there, where his body is – right this minute.'

'I can't. It isn't possible. I wish I could.'

'I hope the fuck you rot in Hell.'

'I am.'

He finds Hennessy irritating and somewhat obnoxious. Too much in your face.

Jimmy is dark and brooding when he returns, drawing on a cigarette and exhaling as though to fog the hurt in his eyes.

Finally, he says, 'Around here?'

'I think I should tell you this now – here, Tyre and Beirut – they are the three places I was told of.'

'A grand tour? Jaesus, Khalil . . .'

Khalil shrugs, 'None of the three might be the right place. No promises.'

'I don't buy everything you're telling me, Khalil – I want you to know that.'

'And I don't either,' Hennessy says, 'and I'm the most gullible fucker you can meet.'

Khalil wags a finger, his eyebrows knitting, 'Listen, both of you – let us be clear – I am trying to help you. I can leave this moment – walk off and—'

'Off? You can barely hobble around the fucking place as it is,' Hennessy says.

'Why do you use bad language all the time, Hennessy – I am Lebanese and speak better English than you, I also speak a little French, and of course, Arabic. Why do you say fuck all the time – don't you know any Irish? *Conas ata tu? Ana mhaith?*'

'It's got to do with my mood – and when I'm in the company of liars.'

'And so how is it you can live with yourself?'

Jimmy uses his hand like an orchestra conductor, 'Quit it, you two – come on, let's have a search – Khalil, give us a general area.'

'The garden – stick to the garden.'

Hennessy glares at Khalil who shakes his head. The man knows a ruse when he spots one. Knows a wild-goose chase. Knows Khalil – all on the strength of what he has heard today and from buying a faulty radio some years ago.

'You know how this works, Khalil?' Hennessy says.

'What works?'

'The fucking dog.'

'No.'

'When training them they bury pigs of different ages and

210

sizes over different time periods in graves of varying depths –
the reason they use pigs is that of all the animals, including
your average Mister Joe fucking Chimp, the pig's decaying
flesh resembles the human's in a similar state. No wonder
the fucking Yids don't eat pork – I haven't been able to let a
rasher cross my mouth since I heard. So they bring the dog
to a site where the police suspect that there's a dead body or
a mass grave and let the dog off the leash – he goes sniffing
and if he gets agitated and starts scratching madly at a spot,
Bob's your uncle and—'

Jimmy joins in, his tone suggesting that Hennessy has
given an incorrect synopsis, 'Another way, Khalil, is to do
what I am about to do, probe the earth with a spoke, driving
it down into the ground. Usually the people we're looking
for haven't been afforded a coffin. If I hit a hollow spot, perhaps where a coffin or a corpse has fallen in on itself, then I
wriggle the probe, widening the vertical space for Jake to get
a good smell – if he reacts, then we start digging, perhaps
using a mechanical digger – the hollow drain I've excavated
is like opening a door for Jake to see in.'

Khalil strokes his chin, 'It is very like the method used by
rescuers after avalanches.'

'Yes, same principle.'

'What kind of success rate?'

'O.K. In Bosnia, Croatia, yes, these dogs have been quite
successful when searching for mass graves – earthquakes

too, sniffing through the rubble for survivors and also for the dead.'

'Bosnia, Croatia – ah, it is the children I feel sorry for. The bad memories they've to carry through life.'

'I was a child when my father was murdered – not that you need reminding.'

Khalil's fingers increase the tempo around his worry beads. Record laps. Own goal, Khalil. Walked into that, eh, my friend?

'I better get a start – this will take a while,' Jimmy says.

He walks a little distance, stops and stares at the garden.

Hennessy whispers to Khalil that Jimmy is trained to examine visually the site of a suspected grave or graves, every little hump or depression he views in a different light than we would. The same way God would look over your soul to see marks you thought you buried well.

What do they know? Khalil asks himself.

The first examination of the scene by the MP Borge had yielded bloodstains on the ground and scuff marks on the bark where O'Driscoll's feet had kicked in his frantic battle for life.

A desert boot worn by Irish soldiers. The left one removed by someone who wanted both but had failed in the attempt. Possibly denied by lack of time, his busy hands losing out in the surge of others rushing the Irishman to the hanging tree.

The American soldier's body, intact, marked with the shit and piss of his executioners, his own trapped in his camouflage slacks. An eye popped from its socket. His pistol lying on the ground, the bullets emptied from the magazine, unopened letters plucked from his shirt pocket – a gold crucifix around his neck. Left there for photographers, left there to show America what they thought of Uncle Sam.

Borge put it to Khalil that it was very strange that the American's body was left *in situ* and the Irishman's taken.

'Why, Khalil, would that be?'

'I don't know. Perhaps they were afraid that the Irish Government would have withdrawn its battalion – they offered some protection and humanitarian assistance, more than the villagers ever received before their arrival.'

'Why does every bone in me smell a lie?'

'I have no answers.'

Other than blood lust, sheer blood lust – an insatiable lust they were desperate to slake.

If they had left Borge at his job, then perhaps . . .

Perhaps the UN, also, had decided that the truth should lie deep in its grave.

The last investigation, seven years after O'Driscoll had gone missing, was carried out as more of an administration exercise, gathering documents and half-heartedly following cold trails, all done to appease the insurance people, who pay out after a person has been missing for seven years but only after evidence is produced to prove that a thorough investigation has taken place.

But even if the investigators had little of Borge's zeal and skill, they still managed to find O'Driscoll's FN rifle. It was discovered in a house that the Israelis had shelled on the outskirts of At Tiri village. Sifting through the debris the weapon showed up in a basement and was originally thought to be one of a pair of Nepalese rifles stolen from Camp Trishul, Nepbatt HQ. They concentrated on Irishbatt where the serial number matched that in a stores log. For a while there was a renewed flurry of interest but it petered out when the trail turned colder than before. When tongues like Khalil's didn't wag.

That is all they know for certain.

The man O'Driscoll is dead.

His rifle is found.

Nothing else.

They know so little that they are depending on the words of an old man to help them unearth a corpse from a grave.

Yes. There is a grave but not of the sort they could ever imagine.

'Are you coming to have a look?' Hennessy says.

'I can see from here.'

'Nothing to get excited over, eh?'

'Go away, Hennessy – I am not a well man.'

Hennessy mutters and makes for Jimmy, stands beside

him with his arms folded – a genie about to grant three wishes.

Khalil looks at his fingernails, neatly clipped and free of dirt. Tobacco stained, the top of his small finger missing, taken away in his younger days by a colleague's careless mishandling of a cement block on a Beirut building site.

How the finger hung on by a thread – blood and bone and flesh showing through burst white skin – dirt under a nail he would never have to clean again.

The pain.

When Daoud asked what happened to it, he said an Israeli sniper took aim from 2km away and shot it clean off.

'Cool, Khalil – that's cool.'

'Losing your finger isn't cool, Daoud.'

'No, but the shot was.'

Khalil turns his attention to Jake, his nostrils close to the ground, sniffing the holes Jimmy had fashioned with his probe. An insulated probe designed to protect him from electric shock.

The sun is strong, too strong to stay under for any length of time.

There is nothing buried here, Jimmy, spare your dog's nostrils.

I owe your father my silence.

Jake starts pawing frantically beside the small mole mound of earth Jimmy has dug away.

No.

It's not possible.

Hennessy looks over his shoulder and beckons Khalil with a wave.

Khalil stirs himself.

Jimmy is shovelling clay away, the earth red and smelling fresh. Jake nibbles on his reward, a pig's ear. Hennessy spits on his hands and rubs them together.

'Give me the shovel, Jimmy – come on, I'll be quicker.'

A few minutes is all it takes for the excitement to sizzle away – the goat isn't long dead, the maggots at work.

'Fuck!' Hennessy says.

'A goat,' Jimmy says.

'A goat,' Khalil confirms.

Later, back at the rear of the cruiser they untab colas Hennessy hands them from the icebox.

'Fucking disappointing, that,' he says.

'Yeah,' Jimmy agrees, smoothing a patch of earth with the ball of his foot.

'Yes,' Khalil says.

Jimmy says, changing tack for mind relief, 'The last time I was in Lebanon I made several attempts to get here, but the operational situation was such, that—'

Hennessy cuts in, 'Yeah, that's the year the Hezbollah were elected into government. They've gotten bolder since then and their attacks are well planned. The Yids are at nothing trying to hang on to this fucking place – not unless they use brute and unrestrained force.'

Khalil says, 'They are more worried about the fledgling Palestinian State. For sure it is an autonomous region the Palestinians will have, but for all intents and purposes we are seeing the birth of a new Palestine and the Israelis are fearful of where this can lead. Everything will hinge on Jerusalem – Jerusalem is the children's favourite sweet, the one no one wants to share. No, a state within a state cannot work.'

Jimmy wipes his forehead with his forearm, 'I suppose we better get going – we'll stay in Tyre this evening and start work in the morning – first thing, Khalil?'

'Yes, fine, first thing.'

I owe your father my silence.

20

In his billet at Tyre MP Detachment, a Unifil outpost stationed within Hassan Burro Lebanese Army barracks,
Jimmy sips at a glass of red wine during a pause in writing
up his journal. Today's exercise was a wash-out. A magpie in
rifle range terms.

Jake's working well the sole positive aspect.

Still, there's Tyre tomorrow and then Beirut the following
day. Why does he feel that the old man is lying?

Hiding something?

Economical with the truth — is that it?

Tom thinks it's all three. Then, he is suspicious of everyone.

Tom is exercising Jake around the barracks before putting
him into an air-conditioned office for the night. It's important that drug and search dogs have air-conditioning to

prevent the Lebanese dust clogging their sense of smell. That's why the kennels in MP Coy are the envy of those humans in billets who have to rely on fans to keep cool. Sometimes, to escape the heat of the night, the dog handlers bunk down with their charges.

Khalil is staying at the Phoenician Hotel in the Maronite Christian Sector, facing the small fishing harbour. He was mostly quiet on the journey to Tyre, looking out the window at the sea. Examining his conscience? Good, if that's the case, good.

Jimmy's room is one of six in a prefabricated building that shows wear and tear. The office block is of stone construction with a corrugated roof. The Dogface, Sergeant Ollie Nordvik, said that the Lebanese Army are pushing for the MPs to move into the UN compound, the old customs post, on the Tyre seafront. They're getting their act together, recruiting and rebuilding, and want to maximize all available and potential space in camp.

Changes. Lebanon is changing, becoming a nation again, the fragments being pieced together – its earth has soaked up enough spilt blood.

Only the other day, Nordvik said, he saw two platoons of trainee gendarmes running in block formation, wearing grey and black disrupted military pattern uniforms and red berets and lanyards – up the Hippodrome road they went – by the bridge from where you can see the Roman road and archway, the Byzantine City of the Dead. A steep climb, eh, Jimmy?

'Yeah, Ollie.'

'Me in the Patisserie Canaan watching them go by – feeling guilty at the cakes I'd eaten – I've put on a stone since I came to Lebanon. When I go home to Norway on leave my wife and children will give me a hard time.'

After completing his entry in his journal, Jimmy takes to his bunk and slips under the green mosquito netting. An hour's rest and he'll drive into town to meet Khalil, bring him for dinner somewhere. Best to leave Tom here because he rises the old fella's blood pressure.

When he told Tom of his attentions his lips crimped, 'I'm all for the truth coming out by whatever means – and hang the fucking consequences.'

Jimmy glared at him until Tom realized that his choice of words was unfortunate. He coloured, cheeks suffusing with tiny purple veins, 'Jimmy, I'm some bollocks – sorry.'

Jimmy turns on his side in his bunk, breathes in and then out. He thinks of home.

The biting loneliness he feels at being away from his wife and child.

His thoughts shade to the day he sat in the living room playing with a wooden cavalry fort. It had troopers in navy jackets, gold striped blue trousers, black boots, peaked forage caps. Horses with blankets bearing the 7th Cavalry motif – real flakes of straw in the stables. He answered the knock on the front door. To find a man in military uniform, a jeep outside the garden gates. The officer sombre faced as though all his worst nightmares had come home to roost.

'Is your mammy home, son?'

She was.

He can never forget that sudden change. From a house full of warmth to an arctic emptiness. Restless. Time to see Khalil. It's a little early. But fuck him.

21

The late afternoon pain isn't so bad – tolerable. There is no clutching of his stomach, no tears bleeding, no grimacing so hard that he feels his face is going to fracture.

The hotel is old and neglected – o's missing from its green neon sign – Ph enician H tel – the façade's white paint blistered in places, primed to burst. The lounge's wine coloured carpet shows its bones of twine, ground so by constant foot traffic, possibly a third generation hand-me-down from a classier establishment. New but old when brought here.

The smell of emulsion mingles with dust and dry rot. Certainly, O'Driscoll is not trying to bribe or impress the truth from him – there is a finer establishment than this south of Tyre, The Rest House, a four star beach hotel – typical of Lebanon – nothing to cater for the masses falling between rich and poor. You are either of one class or the other.

This hotel is a six dollars a night place, breakfast and cockroaches inclusive. Though at least the bed linen is fresh, the room clean, the view through the French window breathtaking – the sea a rippling blue carpet, mosaiced with small colourful fishing vessels and a rusting hulk that juts above the water line.

When O'Driscoll left Khalil at the hotel he said the room was booked and paid for and that he would drop by this evening and collect him for dinner. O.K.?

Khalil said that was fine provided he left Hennessy in barracks.

He took his key from an old woman who sat behind Reception chewing on a mint leaf, turning it in her mouth in the way of a camel – indolent, insolent and with the hint that at any moment she might bite. She had many wrinkles and tired grey eyes, the whites yellow.

'Room Fourteen,' she said, handing over a key.

Climbing the stairs a great weariness sat on Khalil's shoulders and his heart started to palpitate. He staggered towards and sat on the edge of the bed. Eased off his flip-flops, noticed and admired the sea view for the first time and lay back, shut his eyes and surrendered to sleep.

He wakes before seven and counts the hours he has slept. Two, and ten minutes. His mind, body and soul needed that respite. These days good solid sleep comes in snatches, the way a soldier rests during battle, huddled in his foxhole, it is so with him – short breaks from a battle, a losing battle.

Khalil remains lying in the darkness – indistinct radio voices in the next room, a row between a couple in another. The radio voices lowering as the ears prefer the option of live entertainment.

Things crash. A fall of cutlery and crockery.

He has no money for her.

She promised her mother some money.

She needs money.

He says tomorrow.

She says tomorrow never happens.

He promises that it will. So full of conviction he silences her and himself.

Promise, he says, promise. Soothing voice.

Silence.

The radio voices rise to their former indistinct level.

The man is right about one thing – tomorrow comes. You can't roll it back.

Khalil fingers sleep crust from his eyes and eases himself into a sitting position, afraid of stirring the sleeping dragon in his belly.

He inhales a deep breath – he reeks of perspiration – foul sweat – piss, medicine and poison – leaky orifices, eyes remaining rheumy for longer spells.

He is falling in on himself – an old building going to ruin.

He shits and cleans himself and an hour later he smells like he has not wiped himself.

There are positive arguments for dying in the whole of your health.

Khalil stands and pads to a walnut dresser, its drawers an ornate handle short of a complete set. He rings Reception, looking for a line out. He sits and listens to the call ringing and ringing.

'Hello?'

Daoud.

'Daoud, well, boy, what did you do today?'

'We counted things like you said.'

'Any problems?'

'You had a lot of stuff to count. Loads of things, Khalil, we even counted stuff Adeeba said you won't be able to give away.'

'We'll see – is Adeeba there?'

'No, she is still in the shop – Zarifa brought me up to eat dinner.'

'Put Zarifa on – good boy – see you soon.'

'Sure thing, Khalil – Zarifa!'

He waits. The connection so clear he can hear his wife's approaching footsteps.

'Khalil – how did things go?'

'How do you think?'

'Khalil, please?'

'No.'

'At least talk to Adfal – will you? See what he thinks – he might confirm your decision.'

Khalil sucks in air through his teeth. Adfal is Zarifa's older brother. He lives in the Kadisha Valley, near Bcharre, north of Beirut, employed as a handyman and administrator by the Lebanese and administrator Maronite Order. Deir Mar Elisha, four chapels and a monastery that were hewn into the side of a cliff in the fourteenth century and are reached by a steep winding road from the peak of the valley on the south side.

Chapel-caves. Manacles fitted to the walls where they used to chain the insane deposited at the Order. Obsolete, of course. Nowadays, it is drugs that do the chaining. Sometimes chaining isn't necessary. The mind does that for itself.

'Zarifa, me talk to Adfal? I haven't spoken to him in years. He is a peculiar man.

His eyes dance in his head.'

'He is in Sidon tonight.'

'How do you know?'

'I rang the Order – they told me.'

Yes, Zarifa keeps in touch with her family. It is good not to abandon blood.

'He visits Sidon once a month, stays at the Hotel d'Orient on Rue Shakrieh.'

'What in Allah's name brings him there?'

Zarifa's silence tells him.

'I see,' Khalil says, his tone indicating that she need say no more.

He bites his lower lip after saying his goodbyes to Zarifa. It would do no harm to speak with Adfal. He might have some news for him. Though, Adfal is not usually a talker, not a man for giving advice. Dark clouded face keeping the lid on murky secrets. He could mime a dead man, so straight his features.

In Sidon, thirty-five minutes away – visit?

What harm can it do?

Ask him?

Straight out – what does he think? He could kill your doubts.

How many times has he met Adfal since . . .?

Never? Once? Think. Allah, never. And so there was never a word about the favour Zarifa requested of him. The one he acceded to.

Khalil drums his fingers on the table, picks up the phone – books a cab.

He waits in the lounge drinking tea, after leaving a note at Reception for O'Driscoll to the effect that he will meet him here in the morning – sorry to have passed up on the meal. Tomorrow evening? Inshallah.

The taxi driver is a thin man, talkative until he realizes that Khalil isn't in the mood.

Drives past the UN compound, towards the roundabout

at the entrance to the city, veers left, taking the Sidon road, the smell of lamb roasting on a vertical spit cutting in through the space Khalil left in his window.

In Sidon, 40 km north of Tyre, the driver edges left off Rue Faker ad Din, into the old town, finding the Hotel d'Orient above a tiny baggage shop, not far from a Muslim cemetery. An ancient sign on the first floor announces its location – six rooms, a shared bathroom with cold water, extra for a hot shower, an old man says.

Khalil had sent the taxi driver away, instructing him to return in two hours.

'I'm looking for a man, Adfal—'

'He is in his room – I will call him for you,' the old man says. Arthritic in his movements. 'Is he expecting you?'

'No.'

'Who should I say is calling?'

'Khalil, Zarifa's husband.'

The old man frowns, picks at his lower lip.

'It's O.K. – he is not with my wife or daughter – you can call him.'

The old man nods and smiles. Relieved.

Khalil moves into the restaurant. A scattering of circular tables with Sidon's crusader sea castle printed on oilcloths. He draws out a chair and sits down, orders Lebanese coffee for two from a young woman – takes the proffered menu.

Adfal strolls in. A thin, hard man with piercing brown

eyes. He wears grey slacks, the belt frayed near the buckle, a short-sleeved navy shirt, a Ben Sherman leather watch. His silvery hair strung through with dwindling black. His features lean and craggy. Chiselled so by conscience pangs?

Khalil rises to his feet, is ushered down by Adfal's gestures for him to remain seated.

A smile on Adfal's face is as rare as a spell of peace in the Holy Land. In him the source of a smile is as long dried as a wadi bed. Adfal's lips are tightly drawn, the muscles moving in the joints of his cheeks.

'This is a surprise, Khalil. After so long.'

'I hope I didn't interrupt—'

'No – I have reached the shores of old age in good health and with a healthy sexual appetite – I never married, Khalil, so I bask in the company of loose women, pay them for their services and then we wash ourselves of each other.'

'I thought the Hezbollah got rid of all things seedy – I know they moved a gay hairstylist out of Sidon – he ended up in Mingi Street.'

'He must have been flamboyant in his dress, outgoing.'

'Atab is, I suppose, excessively expressive.'

Khalil pours coffee into miniature cups and helps himself to a cigarette from the pack of Lucky Strikes Adfal places on the table.

The wings of a ceiling fan creak and another's flap slowly and silently.

229

Adfal leans across with a lighter.

'Twenty years I've been coming here – there are places in Beirut but nowadays they are full of Russians and Romanians, young girls – I like older women who have been around. Who know their job.'

'It's good to know what you want.'

'It is – my current partner is a Filipino – decent woman. I know nothing of her life apart from the fact that she is grateful for my money and is proud that I ask for her ahead of others.'

'You are still employed by—'

'Of course.'

'I see.'

'Because I can do many jobs for them as well as any expert I save them a lot of expense. Good plumbers, good electricians, good carpenters – do you know how scarce they are firstly and secondly how much they charge?'

'I've heard.'

'Not to mention my silent tongue. A priceless thing.'

A young woman appears like a hawk at Adfal's shoulder, pen poised over notepad.

He orders *sayyadieh*, a fish, delicately spiced, served with rice in an onion and tahini sauce. Khalil chooses likewise.

'And a carafe of red wine, please, Suzanne, the house wine,' Adfal adds.

Turning to Khalil he says, 'So, rarely seen and seldom

heard from brother-in-law, what gives me the pleasure?'

'After the meal.'

'Zarifa says you haven't much time left.'

'Not much.'

'She tells me that Jimmy's son has come to look for him.'

'After the meal – I will ask you then.'

'There's no need to wait, Khalil – I know what it is you want.'

'You do?'

'Yes, to appease your conscience – to tell you that it would be all right for the son to see his father. Or not.'

Khalil nods, settles his cigarette in the chipped gully of an ashtray.

Adfal sits up, pinches the tip of his nose between thumb and forefinger, 'But first, Khalil, all this time you never ask for him. Not once. And now. Now, look at you.

A disgrace to your name. If he were dead – would that make you settle in yourself?'

'No.'

'He is well.'

'Well?'

'He eats, drinks, shits and pisses – he walks, waters plants.'

'But?'

'His eyes are distant, his mind a desert, the rope mark around his neck still clearly visible. His voice is gone –

missing ribs – missing his left foot which had to be amputated shortly after his arrival – missing his right ear, half blind in one eye, his nose a blob of flesh showing only one nostril. He is living and yet dead.'

'I was leaning towards allowing the son to meet his . . .'

Khalil's words fall away as he realizes their pointlessness – after what Adfal has just told him, how could he even consider arranging such a meeting?

'I have done a favour for my sister – brought him from the dead, taken care of him – he has a small job gumming the flaps of the envelopes the Order sends out.'

'Never a word?'

'No. He doesn't even know his own name. We call him Jimmy. But we could call him any name, anything and he would still respond.'

'Doctors?'

'Once, we had a specialist staying in the monastery on a retreat – he examined him – said his brain had been deprived of oxygen for too long and the injuries to his head and body should have been enough to kill him – he must have had some special reason to live.'

'Surely if he can hear and respond, then—'

'A donkey can hear and respond – probably better than Jimmy.'

'I—'

'I won't advise you, Khalil – this thing should not have

happened to Jimmy – better he had been killed back then and not dragged back into this world.'

'A boy saved him.'

'No, no he didn't, Khalil – he didn't save him at all.'

Khalil ponders this for moments.

Voice.

Why the doubts, Khalil? What is it you said? Let me see. Yes – you said something about owing a father a certain silence.

'What can I do, Khalil? Plunder a skeleton from the monastery's crypt – dress him in an Irish uniform, put his blue beret on his ribcage, slip his ring on his finger, rope his dog tags about his hand – leave the skeleton without its head because they'd check dental records?'

'If I thought it would work I would ask it of you – but the sergeant is too clever. He knows without having proof that something is not right about the whole story – a skeleton will hand him proof – forensic science will rule the skeleton out as being that of his father. Then, Jimmy will keep digging.'

'And of me. My position. Have you considered that? I doubt it. If my employers find out that I've kept a Unifil soldier in the Caves of the Mad, instead of the Syrian imbecile I said he was, what do you think will become of me? I'm not fool enough to believe myself totally indispensable.'

'What about your priceless thing? Your silent tongue?'

The anger that swarms into Adfal is of tidal proportion. He seizes Khalil by the throat using one hand, and points a finger in his face with the other, 'Don't be smart. You. My sister asked me for a favour those years ago and she is family and she is a good woman. You, you Mister, should show respect for what I did for her.'

The tidal wave diminishes faster than it appeared. Khalil massages his throat.

Adfal is a strong man. Well practised at what he had just done.

'Eat your food, Khalil.'

Khalil says he will not bring the Irish to Bcharre. He understands.

Later, he takes the taxi home – the visit to Adfal not an exercise in uselessness. He knows now for sure that father and son must never meet. Never. No doubts, no guilt. No more wavering, no uncertainty. A pity Jimmy can't understand the question – 'Do you want to see your son?' A pity. It is hard to be unkind to young Jimmy – he is likable and his mission is admirable. Nevertheless, there is no way Adfal would allow such a meeting to take place. To persist . . .

Khalil's fingers rest on his throat. Don't even think about what would happen to Jimmy Senior.

The driver takes the coastal route, engaging the Beirut road and then looping back for Tyre along the seafront, the spotlights on the sea castle a ghostly yellow in the bright moon and starlight.

In his hotel room he listens to bed springs squeaking and a woman moaning, her man promising her all the money in the world.

Sweet nothings.

22

Khalil's eyes flicker open. Sunlight filters in through the slatted blinds, carrying agitated dust motes in its beams and throwing black prison bars across his sheet. The motors of fishing vessels – the few late to kick in are drowning out the ones already heading to catch the early fish.

As the throbbing of sea traffic lessens the thrumming of road traffic increases. The shower is hot but there is no spray – so he is hosing instead of showering. After dressing in his slacks and fresh shirt he rings Zarifa on his mobile and reminds her that he'll be home early Thursday morning to open the shop. Last shopping in Khalil's, he tells her – perhaps we should provide some refreshments – what do you think?

'I've already thought of all that, Khalil.'

'Good – thanks, Zarifa.'

'Adfal said you met each other.'

'And?'

'He agrees with you.'

'Could he not have told you that in the first place?'

'No. He is suspicious of phones – always thinks there is someone listening in – he is paranoid – ultra careful of what he says.'

The Aussies go walkabout – the Lebanese go wordabout.

'He confirmed what I had been thinking – righted my listing thoughts.'

'I still think, Khalil, that—'

'That I should allow the son to meet a living ghost?'

'It is what he wants. It is what he prays for.'

'No. He prays to find his father's remains.'

'Isn't it the same thing? Also, he might be pleased to learn his father is not dead.'

'He is dead, woman! You don't understand.'

'Don't woman me – he is not dead – he lives. He is damaged but alive.'

'Ach, what's the point in trying to explain things?'

'It's not your fault that his father is the way he is.'

Is it not?

'Zarifa – if Allah worked a miracle and let Jimmy form a thought and utter a sentence – he would say that his son is not to see him.'

'Khalil, let him bring his father home, please?'

'No!'

He hangs up, severing her attempt at placation.

He slips his new tunic over his clothes, takes his pills, one after the other, massages his ribs, polishes off his bottle of still water, exorcises phlegm from his lungs and dabbing a tissue to his mouth, proceeds to join the others in the foyer, his travel bag in his hand.

Hennessy sits with his legs crossed, says Jimmy has gone for a crap. Some fucking Lebbo place poisoned him. Continuing, he says, 'Where did you get to last night?'

'Out.'

'I know you were out – Jimmy called for you, you know?'

'I left a message for him, so he wasn't delayed.'

'He wanted to have a chat with you.'

'We can talk today.'

Hennessy grunts, draws to his feet and says he is going to check on Jake.

'Ah, Major, dog to dog – how lovely.'

'Yeah, but at least he doesn't give me fleas.'

'Fleas would be wasted on you.'

Khalil watches the Irishman gradually disappear from view as he descends the flight of steps.

We certainly bring out the worst in each other.

Jimmy strolls across the tiled floor. Ghastly looking.

'I ate something last night – I need two arses I have it so bad.'

'Where did you eat?'

'Oh some fucking place, Khalil, I don't know, near the crusader ruins.'

'Restaurant Tanit – usually excellent.'

'Yeah, usually, really?'

'So, what are your plans?'

'I'll be O.K. – are we digging around Tyre today?'

'Not so far away.'

'I should be O.K.'

The Tyrian air smells of exhaust fumes, roasting lamb and chicken, and of various spices brimful in hessian sacks. Hennessy talks.

Talks of his previous trips in Lebanon. How in 1978 they washed and shaved themselves with cola. He was with poor Dunny who died during a soccer match in 1981. Never forget the day – honest to Christ – fittest man around – MP Coy were playing the fucking Swedes in the first round of the Unifil Championships – getting slaughtered we were – eight nil – Dunny like a wasp trying his heart out, keeling over. That was fucking sad. He dying and we fucking laughing because we thought he had hit the ground looking for a penalty.

He lay there, still, his eyes open, the cuts on his legs fresh, socks rolled down over his shinguards, boots missing a moulded stud, the perspiration drying on him. It had to be a gag – the fuckers in Camp Martin were always pulling them. But.

And Kinky Sludds, the medic, shot himself the same year. Got a Dear John from his wife who said she was leaving him for his best friend, that they'd been seeing each other for a year – doing it everywhere, every chance they got. Kinky never copped on it was an April Fool's trick and shot himself in the knee so he'd be medically repatriated.

Got promoted afterwards – fucking weapons instructor now – I ask you – army life is full of contradictions.

Khalil is only half listening. He is concentrating on the road, on the watch out for a sly little turn off to the right, easily missed. The narrow road will bring them to a field of olive trees and a half field full of old car wrecks. He will indicate a point and let Jimmy do his futile trick with his dog. Ignore Hennessy.

It's hard. His voice is loud and deep. He sings well, Khalil has heard, ballads and country and western songs. Christy Moore and Randy Travis – two of Jimmy's favourites, too. He plays a cassette in the cruiser sometimes, volume lowered.

Said his father thought Moore was the best thing going, before he had even started to climb the ladder to success.

Hennessy takes the silence in the cruiser as a cue to continue his chronology of Lebanon tours.

'Didn't get back here then until 'eight-five – MP Coy – I was fucking delighted to avoid serving in the mountains – I hate Tibnin – no bleaker place – HQ – the beach at my back door, no woman harping at me, working a seven to three shift, weekends free – paradise – if it wasn't for the fucking Lebanese and other foreigners in the place that's what it would have been – paradise.

'I had a Nepalese Major on detachment in Nahariya – the most useless fucker God ever put on earth. You had to tell him a dozen times to do something – in the end it was always quicker to do the fucking thing yourself. His English – someone would ring the detachment and he'd say Hello and put down the phone – he couldn't string four sentences together. Honest to Christ, that lad broke my heart. I'd a Ghanaian sergeant called Daniel. The day I took over from a Fijian Dogface – it was a Sunday, Jaesus, when I think about it – I spent the whole day turning away Daniel's whores – he was like a magnet to them – really – a gas ticket he was – picked up a bad dose of VD.'

'Turn here, to the right,' Khalil says.

They descend a steep decline, taking a series of turns, driving through narrow streets with electricity wires crisscrossing from roof to roof, segmenting the clear sky.

Windows eyeball each other. The Market Square is a little broader, a little wider, with several roads branching away. Children stand huddled in small groups, old men play backgammon, all stare.

Khalil waves at them and then aims his finger at a road that 100 m on, away from the stares, gives way to a dirt track.

'Here – a scrapyard – has been for years, longer than I

care to remember – this is where I heard your father was buried.'

Khalil speaks the truth – he has heard it from many sources who asserted themselves so strenuously that they almost convinced Khalil. Listening to them in his shop over a water pipe with their versions of the truth at a time when the hangings and the severed noose were fresh news. A dependable thing about the troubles was that a newer atrocity switched the limelight, ageing news quicker than time would have done.

And unless a person is directly touched the memory of each one dries as quickly as blood in the sand.

People convince themselves of things – follow their own or someone else's flight of imagination.

'Are you fit for this, Jimmy?' Hennessy asks.

'Yes, of course – I've waited a long time – can't quit now.'

Khalil steps out, rubs his hands, 'In the embankments behind the yard – take care because sometimes they are home to wild dogs, snakes and wild pigs. The dogs can be dangerous.'

'I've a shotgun, Jimmy – we use it for pest control – used to, actually, until the Poles started shooting people instead of dogs and cats with it.'

Khalil walks a short way from the cruiser. Jimmy is tying Jake to the hitch, talking to him, filling his dish with water. Hennessy chambers shotgun cartridges. There is nothing here for him to find and yet I let them search. I do this in order to make Jimmy feel as though he has tried his living best to find his father's remains – I was unwise to be so charitable. At the start I should have said, 'No, I know nothing of what you speak of – I am dying, leave me alone.'

I didn't.

Had the disease eating away at me so preoccupied my mind that I made a wrong decision?

Yes, there is that.

There is also the fact that you want to spill the truth, you want with all your heart to open the door to a secret. And what is stopping you?

Guilt?

No.

Fear?

No. Yes. A little.

Fear of what? The son's pain and anguish mingled with a peculiar relief at seeing his father?

No. It is what the father might see, might come to understand. That is my fear. And my debt is to him. And it is not redeemable.

They glide by him, the two men, not a word passing their lips. Coming to a spot Jimmy draws up short, scans the area, first with his naked eye and then using binoculars. They move into the scrapyard where Jimmy climbs atop a blue Peugeot and studies the grassy banks that in peacetime were rifle butts for the Lebanese Army.

The dogs start barking. Hungry mongrels – about five – dogs showing their ribs and general manginess, baring their teeth.

Jake acts up, on his feet, snarling and barking, straining at his leash.

The dogs start running, advancing. Khalil hastens to the car and climbs inside.

Notices that the hatch at the back is open.

Shit.

Jake.

The shotgun roars once, then twice. Whelps and shrieks from the dogs as the pellets strike home.

A black and white dog lies dead on the ground, near a Volkswagen, a wounded animal's yelps are still loud, but he is out of view, losing himself in the scrap city, going home to die. The other dogs are fleeing in all directions.

Jimmy gets down, uses his probe as a walking stick as he breaks for the embankment, while Hennessy heads this way, stopping to prod the dead dog with the nose of the shotgun's barrel.

'I thought you were dying,' he says, reaching the cruiser.

'I—'

'You took off like a sprinter.'

'I—'

'Like lightning you were.'

'Fear is a great kick-start.'

'I thought you only looked yellow.'

'In the words of a great Irish Chief – go to be fucked, Hennessy.'

Jake keens.

When Jimmy returns a half-hour later he says he's probed two locations. Could be a dead animal, might be nothing at all. Taking Jake's lead off the hitch he tells Khalil there's a pig's ear in the glove compartment, will he give it to Jake if he goes active?

If he's not rewarded for finding something he'll be confused – not very fair. Sniff for your own the next time. I'd ask Tom but maybe we need to keep him posted with the shotgun.'

'Ah, Jimmy, leave Khalil – he's feeling a little yellow – that sprint has him beat.'

Khalil says, 'I'll be fine.'

He doesn't feel fine. The last time he ran? Allah, about twenty-five years ago, after a car bomb detonated in Rue Hamra, Beirut. His knees feel like jelly. His lungs are in shock, scalded from the air that has touched depths not reached for an age.

He watches Jimmy remove Jake's lead, and prepares himself for the chill silence, the heated words that will follow another disappointment.

23

They were held up in Beirut bound traffic. A long tedious crawl into the city, inching past an oil refinery, closed up hotels, the airport, trundling a right turn, easing over potholes, constant tooting of horns, the dust and grit caused by the construction of new roads and new buildings, the traffic flow squeezed into a single lane, motorbike cops whirring about like cowboys herding cattle, fearful of a stampede.

Reaching Unifil House, on the outskirts of the city, Jimmy parks in a space that faces a small Syrian tented encampment. Khalil takes a keen interest in his surroundings now that the journey has ended.

Unifil House is a converted apartment block that houses all the UN's administration wings in Lebanon under the one roof. The MPs have two apartments on the sixth floor –

their main tasks are to control traffic during twice daily inward and outward flights at the UN Helipad in Beirut International Airport, routine investigations, including traffic accidents involving Unifil and local Liban vehicles, and to escort the BLO, Beirut Liaison Officer, to the various functions he is routinely invited to attend.

'Who's in charge here?' Jimmy asks, at the back of the cruiser, pulling his shirt from his spine, the dried perspiration a weak glue.

'The BLO is, I suppose, he's an Italian Colonel – the lads call him Mussolini,' Tom says.

'No Dogface then?'

'There is – a Pole, Sokolowski, a Warrant Officer Three, a good man.'

'He won't mind us staying?'

'Not at all – but Khalil can't – we can drop him to the Concorde Hotel later – it's O.K., not a dump like that other kip you booked him into.'

He looks at Khalil as he speaks. Khalil detects a softening of attitude. Why there should be a shift is hard to fathom. Perhaps Hennessy comes to grips with himself at times and his bluntness, his coarse language, repels him enough to try and change his ways and his outlook? It's more probable that Jimmy has had words with him.

In the vestibule, Tom and Jimmy are vetted by Federal Security Guards, a local Lebanese security company, and while they are allowed to proceed, Khalil is told to take a seat in the foyer.

'We won't be long, Khalil – just want to show our faces and settle Jake in,' Jimmy says.

'It is funny how they will let a dog go with you and not me.'

Tom says, 'Don't look at it like that – the dog is part of Unifil – has his own ID card number and all. He's one of us.'

'No amount of numbers makes a dog more of a human than a human.'

Jimmy hands the lead to Tom, 'Look after him – I'll drop Khalil to his hotel.'

'You don't know the way.'

'Khalil does, I'm sure.'

'I do, yes.'

Khalil stiffens as he rises. The pain shoots through him, forcing him back onto his seat.

He moves gingerly to the cruiser, assisted by Jimmy who cups his elbow down the steps. Tom says he will ring the Concorde and make sure everything is in order.

Asks if Khalil needs a doctor.

Khalil shakes his head. Wants to speak, to show that he appreciates Hennessy's turn of character, but his tongue feels like it is stuck to the roof of his mouth. They pass through the Unifil House gates, downhill, taking a left turn near Beirut Golf Club, swinging into the main flow of traffic heading downtown. Syrian checkpoints every few hundred metres, monitoring not controlling traffic. Jimmy follows Khalil's pointed finger along the Corniche, the fairground and Military Beach, indicating right to proceed uphill past Lord's Hotel. The Concorde Hotel is only a few turns of tyres farther, settled in a corner between the wings of a Y-junction.

Khalil sits in his room, alone. Jimmy has long gone, with directions to Unifil House mapped on hotel notepaper.

He feels a little better, washed and wearing fresh clothes, his pills taken. The rats at his bones quiet for now.

He has called Zarifa and spent some time discussing things with her, about the upcoming sale, the trip to the air-port with Dahab and Daoud on Saturday – he will miss the boy.

'You are quiet in yourself, Zarifa – is something the matter?'

'No, of course not, Khalil.'

'There is, but you can tell me when I reach home.'

'I can't keep a secret from you, can I?'

'No – there is only one of us good at keeping the mouth in his heart locked.'

'Regrettably.'

'Don't start.'

His mobile cut out, no credit – low on battery power – a double kill.

Why didn't she tell him? Must be about Adeeba, who else? Aziz? Possibly.

Watching TV he smokes a hash reefer. Takes a call from Jimmy and tells him he isn't up to dining out, got a rock in his gut, his lungs are rattling like old exhausts ready to fall off, and his ribs – he fears the pain there most of all. Boss of all his other pains. He kills the lights and leaves the curtains deep in their pleats, pushes back the long nets that screen the patio. Undressing he folds his clothes across the back of a chair and climbs into bed, lying on his side, facing the patio and the host of stars in the ink dark skies.

Closes his eyes – his ears begin to deafen towards the city's noises, sleep comes.

Dreams.

Clouds drifting across a mountain range, a breeze blowing stiff in his face – cold, so cold – he is alone yet feels he is not alone – he exists and yet he doesn't exist.

There is no pain.

None.

That is not to say there is no sense of trepidation.

He moves across the scrub grass onto fissured, sun baked earth. Stands on a hard crust of earth. Pans.

An eagle with an enormous wingspan flies low across the plains. The sight fills him with awe – the creature is magnificent – it is quiet, powerful and has an aura of presence.

Skeletons of animals lie strewn about in a freshly ploughed field – worms exiting through gaping eye sockets. A snake weaves its way across the field of bones at great speed. Its hissing like the beat of a train. Its tongue forked, as forked as the stick his father fashioned, a stick he used to pin the head of a snake to the earth and watch it squirm before the fall of his machete.

The eagle has flown out of sight.

He is not aware of his own physical presence.

No arms, no legs, no torso – no feet, no toes to wriggle.

He may well be a Beirut car bomb victim.

A surge of awareness is overwhelming as he realizes that he has,

No tears to bleed

No blood to lose

No eyes to see

No tongue to wound

No ears to hear.

The sun turns blue in a pale sky. Streaks of yellow light are stripes on the mountain flanks – there is a noise – the beating of hooves, coming closer.

How can I hear if I have no ears?

See – if I have no eyes?

Think – if I am dead?

Am I a spirit?

One about to be judged?

The horse is white, pure white – a leather saddle studded with red opals.

The man astride is tall, kindly looking with a goatee beard. Dressed in a blue silk robe with scarlet piping. His eyes are large and round, piercing, the colour of amber.

Smell the horse – oats and hay and dung, leather soap.

See the vapour jet from its flaring nostrils.

A horse ridden hard, as though there had been an appointed time to make.

Extracting a scroll from a quiver of them the man unfurls and holds it like a knight of old about to read a proclamation. The horse lowers its head, scuffs at the earth, a hoof in earnest search for a shoot of grass to chew on.

'You are Khalil Abbas?'

The voice is strong, a soft bellow – the tone accusing.

'Yes.'

The man reads from the scroll – an account of sin by sin.

Khalil realizes they are his. Some are failings he recognizes as his own, others he doesn't recognize but instinctively knows are his.

Finished, the man rolls the scroll and throws it at Khalil. It lands somewhere – it might be at his feet – with a loud thud.

'You are to wait here.'

'Wait here, where is here?'

'These are the Deserts of Pain. Beyond the mountains lies

the Kingdom – its gates closed to you, for now, until you are purged.'

The man raises the reins and urges the horse to the right, about-turning. The beating of hooves fades, the blue sun turns red, the skies darken. The mountains shorn of their gilt.

Suddenly, the mountains fill with ice and snow and protruding rocks appear craggy and formidable – insurmountable.

The bellowing wind is a scythe of ice, relentless and bitterly cold – pushes him from the mountain's face.

About him there is barrenness, a red burning plain, not a bush, not a weed, not a cactus – just a vast emptiness. Full of footprints not his own, his yet to join.

He walks. Has feet for the ground to burn, has eyes to see his future, ears to hear the lament of the wind, nostrils to clog with dust, has his heart to know true despair.

Walks.

Pain.

Hunger.

Cold.

Anger.

Shivers and yet is warm.

A craving to see another's face, hear another's voice and hold another's flesh.

Zarifa?

Father?

'Mother?'

Is that her – in the distance? So far away yet he hears her calling, 'Has anyone seen my baby, my Yusef?'

Over and over – a mantra – replaced by a different voice.

'Jimmy? Come home, where are you? You're an awful child, stop hiding.'

He turns and walks away but the lamentations follow – these two voices joined by others, all funnelling into his ears and swirling about inside his head. Filling him with an emptiness, a forlornness.

How is it a man can be so filled with emptiness?

Glint of sun on water.

Again.

Glinting at him. Ah, Allah, some mercy, thank You, thank You!

Lips cracked, face prickling with heat, his throat itching for the flow of the water, he sees Heaven in a tiny pool – clear, clear water – and trees next to it, miniature cedars, as small as bonsai.

Lowers himself to his knees, and dips his hands into the water – ice cold on his hands, too cold to cup and bring water to his lips. Spreads his hands in front of him and eases his belly to the ground, and touches his lips to its surface – a taste of sand he spits out. Climbs to his hunkers and eyes the water as though it has just bitten him. A shimmering mirror surface reflects the dark skies – he recoils in horror from his own reflection. A stitched blob of a nose, a missing eye, a circle of black and blue bruising around his neck. Following his crazed way across the Plain is the rustling of leaves on miniature cedars.

Wakes before the muezzin.

Lies perfectly still so as not to waken the pain. Basks in how it used to be to wake every morning feeling like this.

It is true – health is . . .

The call to prayer pierces his thoughts – a lonely cry reaching across mosques, near-empty streets, hospitals, backyard factories, cemeteries, beyond the waves that lap against Beirut's shores, dying somewhere out to sea, carried there on the shoulders of waves. Laid to rest.

He rouses himself from bed, pondering his dream. A vivid nightmare – his neck itches.

A real dream?

Calls room service and orders coffee and toast.

Famished, but why eat what can't be kept down? Toast is enough – a Pony Express rider trying to make it through Indian territory.

He takes his order onto the balcony and sets the tray on a small circular table.

Daylight has broken through, but there is still the quiet of a city just awakening.

Sips at his coffee, adds sugar and stirs, picks at his dry toast.

The dream upset him. He had cried in his sleep, for there were sobs in him when he awakened.

Has he been warned? Has an angel whispered the truth of things to come into his ears? A Scrooge-like visitation of the shape of the future unless he changes his ways?

Bull.

Or as Hennessy would say, 'Shite!'

Is it?

Voice.

Is it, Khalil? Listen to Zarifa.

No.

Listen.

No.

Ah then, see his face in yours when you try to sip at the Pool of Truth.

Khalil rubs his lips, freshens his glass, walks to the parapet and stares across the city.

Today, visit a cemetery where there's not much chance of Jake being successful or even used – too many disturbed graves, bombed in error, of course in error by the Israelis – you can't kill dead people. Not even come close to it. A caretaker who lives at the entrance tells people that when the bombs landed it rained bones on his roof.

Khalil had last been there with Zarifa at her father's

funeral. It was the old man's dying wish to be buried in Baalbek, his home town, but the troubles had prevented that, the region cut off for many months.

Zarifa has since been back to check on her father's remains. He wasn't one of the unfortunate ones – his grave intact, his bones didn't rain.

There was a time after her father died that she used to discuss exhuming his body but she stopped talking about it soon afterwards. She said Adfal didn't approve.

He wanted his father's plot in Baalbek for himself, she said. But Khalil knew that that talk from her was woman spite and no more – Adfal understands, unlike Jimmy, that a proper grave is a proper grave no matter where it is.

Yes, bring Jimmy and Tom and Jake to the cemetery, show them and then go home.

Have your sale, your little party, close the doors on Mingi Street – take to your home on the hill.

Say goodbye to Daoud.

Last days with Zarifa and Adeeba.

Forget about the bloody Irishmen and their dangerous pursuit.

24

What conversation there is on the 120 km journey to Naqoura is terse and sporadic. During a piss stop Tom tells Jimmy that his tongue is on a leash and it's best for him to say nothing lest he says too much. Buttoning his fly Jimmy stares at Khalil, his head lolled against the window, sunken eyes showing an outline of skull to come.

Jimmy's anger smoulders – why won't he tell? What's under the lid he's sitting on?

The old man is aware of Jimmy's hard stare but doesn't acknowledge, his features cast in a mould of pain and dourness.

Jimmy wishes he were a heartless man, for such a man would have wrung the truth from Khalil in that Beirut cemetery – but only a heartless man, a hyena of a man would attack such a stricken creature.

The rusted iron gates at the entrance to the cemetery had been ajar, locked into position by bramble and thorns of Christ that had entwined themselves around the lower regions of the round bars.

Tom stood on the undergrowth, compressing it into a mattress of weed. Turning sideways they edged between the gates, ducking under the sagging link chain. Behind them, Jake barked through the cruiser's small depth of window opening. Drawing up short at the end of a gravel stretch, dotted with islands of weeds, they looked around.

Broken and chipped headstones circled the jagged circumferences of bomb craters. A small wood of silver birch kept company with three low boundary walls, and the remnants of a railing capped the low wall that ran each side of the gates they had passed through.

Choirs of cicadas chirped.

Jimmy saw a lot of depressions during his visual examination. There were no new mounds, nor fresh wreaths nor flowers. It had been a long time since anyone was buried here, in the official plot.

It made no sense to probe the burial area, so Jimmy walked the perimeter, searching for signs – a man-made hummock, a slight depression, anything that might indicate an unnatural disturbance of the soil. If his father was buried here it would have been in a hastily dug grave, not too deep. He could also have been buried in a grave already occupied. That's if he were buried here at all.

A fob exercise.

Or perhaps, Khalil genuinely had nothing more to offer?

Bullshit.

He was there, a key witness. A boy ran and tried to lift the dying soldier's feet, to ease the pressure on his neck by lessening the body weight, screaming that he knew the soldier, that he was a good man.

What happened next? For the umpteenth time what happened next?

They cut him down. Too late, of course.

So they had to put his remains somewhere. Where, where, fucking where?

What the fuck am I looking at? What became of Dad?

A rising breeze, the trees began to dance, a desolate feeling came over him. Didn't he read somewhere that the IRA fed a dead SAS captain into a mincing machine? No body, no crime, no evidence, no trail.

He had landed in Lebanon with too many high hopes – in the first instance he thought that he was simply coming out to collect his father's remains, that identification was a mere formality. He had taken Jake along to practise searching in hot conditions and in case of the unlikely eventuality that the remains he was shown were not his father's. Delusional.

Yet, standing in that cemetery, he felt so close to the truth, had this feeling that it was within his arm's grasp and when

he looked next to him he saw Khalil, and realized for defi-
nite that the old man knew more than he was saying. God,
he did!

Khalil knew!

Accepted, too, that there was no point in probing the
ground – the probe, he told Khalil, can detect different layers
and types of soil, whether or not the soil was recently disturbed. That it is insulated against the risk of electric shock.

A pity there was no such probe for a man's tongue, to test
the shades of truths that rested there.

Khalil stared at him, puzzlement creasing his forehead.
His features like old parchment – brittle and coarse. Like his
nerves – in the early stages of flaking.

'What is it you are really saying?'

'Two things, Khalil, firstly there isn't much point in
searching here and secondly, I want to hear about the things
that you haven't told me.'

Khalil's eyes flickered. Clearly, he had not expected such
directness. But he was quick to compose himself.

'You must give me some time so I can fabricate something
for you.'

'Tell me, Khalil – quit clowning around.'

'Tell you what?'

Tom approached them and as he was about to speak,
Jimmy indicated he should stay out of earshot for another
few minutes.

'So, you read minds and hearts, is that it?' Khalil said.

'No, I have the strongest feeling – it is how a gambler makes his living – instinct and assessment.'

'Not all gamblers are successful.'

'This one is confident. A wager?'

'Wager?'

'I say wager because I don't want to say bribe. You want money, Khalil, how much?'

Khalil's fingernail scratched his worry beads.

'Christ, why won't you tell me? For fuck's sake, all I want to do is bring him home.'

'I—'

'Khalil, if you had a son – if that kid Daoud was your son – he would come looking for you – if the circumstances were the same.'

'And what, Jimmy, should I say next? If I can't tell you the truth there is little sense in telling you anything.'

'You're a liar.'

'You waste your time.'

'It's my time!'

'And mine – so, leave me alone, Jimmy – you are making a wild accusation.'

'Who was the man you were with in Sidon?'

Khalil hid his surprise, 'In Sidon?'

'Yes.'

'He was my brother-in-law.'

'From the Kadisha Valley?'

Khalil angled his chin to the right, as though to avoid a blow, his eyes distant.

'A bribe can yield a lot of information, Khalil.'

The old man? The young waitress? The Filipino whore? Jimmy read the question in the other's eyes.

'A bribe? Why bribe when I could have told you at no cost?'

'Ah, but you didn't.'

'You didn't ask – and what business is it of yours who I meet, who I see? He is a family member who I have not seen for a long time and will not see again – I resent this intrusion of yours.'

'I—'

'I have no more to say – take me to Naqoura now, or I will hire a taxi – this is enough. Enough of this.'

'You—'

'Enough, I said!'

Jimmy pulls up outside Khalil's house. The old man alights and gingerly makes his way up the path to the open front door.

'Not a whisper of a goodbye from him,' Tom says.

'No,' Jimmy says wearily.

'You're finished with the oul fucker, so?'

'I think he's finished with us.'

'How about his old doll – any point in asking her any questions?'

'No – she'd be worse than Khalil.'

'You think?'

'Yeah, I think.'

He eases into gear and edges from the kerb.

In camp he leaves Jake for Tom to feed and put into his kennel. He buys beers and roasted peanuts from a Nepalese barman in the MP Mess and takes them into the bamboo arbour. Late afternoon the camp is relatively quiet. Most soldiers have either gone to the mess or for runs or walks to the border, the UN civilian workers have long crossed over into Israel.

Time to wrap it up, Jimmy. It's all over, done with. The old man isn't going to talk.

Not to anyone in this world.

Visit the Valley, that monastery the Filipino breathed? Speak with Adfal. Roll over another stone.

Time, I haven't much time. My spell in Lebanon almost up – Jake is required for other jobs back home. He has quarantine to get through – then a new owner. Going to break my fucking heart, but . . .

Shit.

I could organize a heliflight to Beirut and be at the monastery in three or four hours.

Sleep on it.

There's only so much I can do and very little if the information isn't accurate or forthcoming. Why bother going –
putting brittle hope and its subsequent disappointment on
my shoulders.

Why didn't I drive there with Khalil?

Kidnap him?

Drastic.

Nonsense ideas. What I should have done was aired the
idea and sussed his reaction.

Slow, too slow on the uptake. Always fucking was.

Some investigator – not switched on at a time when I
needed to be.

If you were paying someone for the service you'd scream
for your money back.

The sun starts to descend, a burning orb touching the
horizon, slowly sinking and two Israeli gunboats specks on
its face, crocodile eyes above water.

'Well, Jimmy, that's that,' Tom says, joining him, taking a
beer off the table and popping it, 'I need this – all angels
have a fall now and then, eh?'

'I was sitting here, eating the arse off myself for being
stupid.'

'Ah, go easy on yourself.'

'I was thinking about that monastery in the Kadisha
valley.'

'The one Sweaty Betty told you about?'

'Yeah.'

'And going there . . .'

'Is another stone to roll over.'

'I can see by you that you're going there no matter what I say.'

'Am I? And you don't think I should?'

'I think you've tried hard enough, devoted enough time of your life – it's time you moved on.'

Jimmy nods, drinks beer and wipes his lips with the back of his hand.

'One more stone, Tom.'

'Errah, then you better roll the fucking thing.'

They drink steadily, constantly, not saying much. Duty personnel drift into the Mess and make tea or coffee, occasionally checking the veranda for a familiar face. Tom smokes cigars, the mild sort that give you a mild sort of cancer, he says.

Tipsy, Tom makes for the bar and returns with more beer and mosquito coils which he affixes to aluminium plinths.

Striking a match he lights the ends of the coils. Tails of fragrant smoke start to rise and spread and become grey blue clouds. He puts one coil on the table and the others on empty tables beside them.

'Mossies, I hate the fuckers – they'd ate you raw if you let them.'

Jimmy appreciates Tom's company. Glad of the beer, too –

it turns his mind to jelly, sort of elasticky, at ease with himself and others – fuck, Khalil's all right, even if he's singing dumb, old fuck. He has his viewpoint, too – his reasons. Fucker.

'That platoon, the one your dad and I served in – we lost a few bodies, we did – time and disease and all fucking that – your dad was the most popular guy in the platoon, the sort who'd keep your spirits up in the worst of situations. Always had a surprise in him. I remember we were stuck in Stranahely Wood on bivvie exercise – we were paired off and told to join our ponchos and make tents. So, we did – it drizzled and then it began to piss rain. Winter, dark early, the rain teemed down in that wood – the smell of pine strong, a washed scent – other guys who didn't pitch their ponchos right ended up bunking down on the beds of trucks. Anyway, your da, when it's my turn for sentry duty – three a.m. – hands me a small bottle of whiskey – when you're wet, bone cold, hungry and staring at two hours of watch duty in the milling rain, the forest floor mucking you above the ankles, ah shit, Jimmy, your da, like – his heart was in the right place, even if he was a bit of a fucking Sergeant Bilko.'

'Tell me, no bullshit—'

'The Sergeant Major doesn't bullshit.'

'Had you ever any close calls here?'

'In the Leb? No. I have a brother who swears he would be

dead now if he hadn't bent down to tie up his desert boot, a round sizzled above his head. Point Five – you can imagine the damage that would do to a fella.'

Jimmy lights up one of Tom's cigar – no cigs left.

'I almost got done in Iraq – you were there afterwards, Jimmy – the fucking mountains. Jaesus. We left the base in Sulaimaniyah, travelling north into the mountains – sheer cliff on one side, sheer drop on the other – narrow road, tight as a laneway.

This fucking boulder right in our path and what does our Iraqi driver decide to do, Jimmy, but drive over the fucking thing. The cruiser went lopsided – I thought we were all fucking goners. The screams of us, Jaesus – the driver got out and moved the boulder, and the Iraqi Liaison Officer climbed in behind the wheel and took off, leaving him there – abandoned him in the middle of nowhere. At the time I thought the dangerous fucker deserved it.'

'I see.'

'Yeah, Jimmy, that's about it, closest call – over a fucking cliff.'

A mosquito breaks the smoke barrier, buzzing through.

Jimmy says, 'I'm hitting the sack, Major.'

'Steady, I'm away, too – seeing as we're to roll over another stone.'

Belches and hiccups escape Jimmy. He places his hand on

Tom's shoulder, 'No, Tom, this one I'll do for myself. I feel you have to.'

'You mean you feel you have to?'

'That's what I said.'

'No, you said, I quote, "I feel you have to," that's what you said.'

'Apologies – I mean I have to.'

Later on, Jimmy turns over in his bunk, catches the vomit in his throat before it rises any farther, makes the cacti patch and vomits – drums dancing in his head as his stomach heaves again. More beating drums, joining in at different pitches, African drums. War drums, crazy drums.

The drums thumping in the background, gathering momentum until the beating is frenzied, wakening him with a dry scream in a dry throat. Wide eyes meeting the black of night.

25

The house is empty. He is a ghost who has wandered in through an open front door, expecting to find everyone and everything as he left them.

Playing at being alive.

The car isn't parked in the drive – Mingi Street? The sale is tomorrow and perhaps they are putting the finishing touches to his shop, allowing friends and neighbours to have first refusal on some of the items. Perhaps?

In the kitchen he eases his holdall to the floor, Cutie meowing at him for milk. He shoos her away.

Jimmy O'Driscoll believes that he knows something. The truth is a mountain that he can see, trek towards and climb – prior to this the mountains were many and their peaks obscured by cloud.

Zarifa's interference!

Voice.

Do you think the truth lies buried forever? Why not wash your hands of the lies and fabrications and state your case?

Opening a cupboard he takes out some painkillers and shoots them home with swigs of bottled water.

Sixty pills a day to keep him going.

Returns to the front door and slams it shut, the knocker clipping a couple of times with the force.

Has he worked hard all his life, rebuilding from nothing, to leave a door open for thieves to enter?

Footsteps above him, hurrying down the stairs, pausing midway, 'Who's there?'

'Dahab! Where is everyone?'

'Khalil – what are you doing home so early? We expected you tonight.'

She joins him in the kitchen. Concern lining her features.

Abruptly he says, 'Never mind that – why was the front door left open?'

'I never noticed. Zarifa was last out – she has taken Daoud to the shop. She said she wouldn't be long.'

He nods, puts the tips of his fingers to his lips – an apology of sorts, silently saying he will take more care in future while birthing his words. Sighs.

'You look tired and you look angry, Khalil.'

'I am tired, very tired.'

'Would you like coffee?'

'No, no. thanks – I will have some juice and retire to bed – I have much to think on. You might send Zarifa up when she comes home.'

'Yes, of course.'

She parts her lips to speak but instead raises her eyebrows.

'You and Daoud, you are all set, all ready for the big adventure?'

'The great escape, you mean.'

'Yes, I mean that.'

'We are ready.'

'Aziz?'

'He thinks we're going to Beirut, to the fun park.'

'How is he treating you?'

No comment.

He takes a leaf of tissue paper from an upright stand on the draining board. Mops his lips. Dahab says she will bring his juice to him, if he wants to head on to his room.

He nods.

The staircase is a mountain. Mount Hermon. His knees ache – if Dahab's eyes were not on him he would drop to his knees to complete the climb.

He needs a shower but hasn't the inclination, the willpower to drag himself to its tray and twist the dial. Anyway, no matter how hot the spray the cold would not leave his bones.

In bed he lies on his back, too weak to sit up and drink the juice Dahab brought him. His eyes flicker open and shut and open and shut.

It is the power of too many painkillers, it is the storm in his innards, it is the unveiling of the truth, the dejection at being found out, that has him in bed, wishing for sleep to come and take him away from all that has happened – three hours' sleep. That will be sufficient rest to enable him to face another day. It is enough because to hope for any more is a fool's wish for the impossible – his next long sleep will be a sleep of the ages. Peaceful – inshallah!

Zarifa calls in late afternoon. Draws the curtains and opens a window, saying there's a sour smell. Then she asks how is he feeling?

'O.K. I am going to wash in a few minutes.'

'You look terrible, Khalil – I should call Dr Frere.'

'No. Later, after tomorrow – no, after Saturday.'

She sits on the edge of the bed, touches his forehead.

'Cold, you're cold, Khalil.'

'On a summer's day, the sun burning – yes, I am cold.'

'How did things go?'

'Not well – O'Driscoll followed me to Sidon, spoke with someone there, has found out where Adfal lives.'

Zarifa places her hands on the side of the bed as though to stop it moving.

'I should not have listened to you, Zarifa – should not have met with Adfal.'

'You should have listened from the very start to me, all those years ago – you should have listened to me before and during this stupid goose chase of yours.'

'No!'

'Yes!'

'Get out, Zarifa! Get out!'

The effort he puts into shouting drains him.

He flops his head onto the pillow. The pillow feels wet and sticky, a sopping sponge, but he doesn't care. Later, he will shower and then he will think some more – she is right, she has always been right.

How does it feel for her – to know she is so right and yet be unable to drive her point home?

Adfal?

Shouldn't he receive a call to alert him that he may have visitors?

Ah, let Zarifa deal with it – she has all the answers.

Always had.

He touches his feet to the floor. Time to get up.

In the kitchen he apologizes for shouting at her, says that she was right – had been all along.

Zarifa hands him a glass of tea.

Apology accepted.

There is iron in her features. Her lips thin.

'I have called Adfal,' she says.

'I suppose he is angry. He is ri—'

'He is afraid of losing his job, of the monks finding out that the Irishman is an Irishman and not the poor deranged Syrian he led them to believe.'

'What will happen?'

She glances at the clock, 'I expect by now, knowing Adfal, it has already happened.'

'No, Zarifa, no.'

He clasps his head in his hands, 'No . . .'

'It has to be.'

'Ring him, tell him not to harm the man, not now – Adfal can live here in this house, with you, if the monks fire him.'

'He can't – I wouldn't have him under the same roof – do you think Adfal has not killed before? He has, men and women and children – what do you think became of the insane in Lebanon during the war? I know Adfal killed those who were difficult to manage – who turned the tap full flow from meagre resources – they had to die.'

'That's murder.'

'Khalil, that's exactly what it was and is – but Adfal and a couple of men like him saw it as sometimes being merciful – O'Driscoll will find nothing.'

'There will be records.'

'No records. He arrived with no name and mingled with others who had no names. A war victim – that's all he is – in this country there are thousands like him – he was a mouth to feed, a body that needed a blanket. A mind, too – but this they could not provide.'

Khalil massages his temples.

'I don't know why Adfal let him live in the first place,' Zarifa says.

'What?'

'I asked him to do the right thing, way back then I asked him to do that – to do the right thing. Neither of you listened to me.'

After some moments of silence, Khalil says, 'Ring him – tell him that he is not to hurt O'Driscoll.'

'You ring him – the number is in the book by the phone and his mobile number, too.'

'I will, I will do it.'

'Don't be a fool, Khalil.'

'A fool?'

'It is not your concern, it never was – you didn't put a rope around his neck, you didn't—'

'I beat him. That night I helped the others bundle him into the back of a car – we thought he was dead – remember – he was dying, perhaps he even died for a few minutes, but he started moaning and moaning and I was in the back with him and something snapped in me and I started to beat him, pummel him with my fists until he quietened – I was sure I had killed him – his moaning frightened me – panicked me. We kept him for a week in Sourb's house – he was a doctor –

he kept him alive, barely – and then I asked you about Adfal, that perhaps . . .'

Pause. 'His moan – I will carry its pitch to the grave.'

'I could never understand why you had that involvement, Khalil, not a sensible man like you.'

'Sensible but cowardly – I was too cowardly to hold my hand up and say, "No." I have often thought about that night, changed everything that happened that night in my mind – I should have taken him straight to a hospital and left him there, telling the doctors I found him on the side of the road. I could have fallen away into the shadows like many others, started my car and left. I had options – instead, when I followed the boy, and they cut the Irishman down, I answered Sourb's call. He called me by name, the way you would speak with a friend, as though it was natural that I should be there with him, hanging people, "Khalil, give me a hand – help us here." I did, and took on his curse, shared the mark on his soul.'

Zarifa says quietly, 'You were caught up in events – you shouldn't blame yourself.'

'I was afraid, Zarifa – I knew what should be done, what should be said and yet said or did nothing – and when I was asked to help them I readily agreed, flying in the face of all I believed – that evening I saw myself as I really was, a coward. Morally and physically I saw deep in myself for the first time. I knew that if my father were alive I would have earned his eternal disappointment. The cancer in me, Zarifa, is a product of that night – for since that night I have had countless nightmares, countless pangs of upset and worry, guilt spearing me when I least expected it – times when I thought of him, his family – I failed him that night, but mostly, Zarifa, I failed myself.'

'You never failed us.'

'Ah, it isn't the time, Zarifa, to comfort me – for you see, I still have the weakness, still the failing – if I had listened to you, showed the man his father, then I would say that at least I had done the right thing this time round, but I didn't – I stood behind the skirt of convenience by telling myself I was protecting the son from the father and vice versa, while in fact the only one I was trying to protect was myself.'

'Khalil – when you die you will not be judged, for you have already judged yourself.'

'No. I have come to know myself. It saves being told.'

'You are not a bad man, Khalil.'

'Sometimes weak men are bad men because of their weakness. And you know me well – you asked me to ring Adfal, knowing full well I would never.'

'Khal—'

'Zarifa – I'm going out back to sit and rest and smoke a water pipe – to drink some arrack.'

'And tomorrow you close the shop – you won't be there if you drink arrack and smoke hashish.'

'Adeeba and you and Daoud—'

'Adeeba is not here.'

Khalil asks, 'When did she leave?'

'Yesterday – Ossie called for her. She went.'

Yes, he supposed it had to happen. Adeeba indicated that it would. She will have his baby and join his second wife – she and Zarifa will be distant – and Ossie will tolerate her and preen her until Zarifa dies and the house becomes Adeeba's and his. And then he will either be kind to her out of habit, in appreciation of where she has brought him, or he won't, and he will kiss her with his fists. The best thing for Adeeba is for him to be killed in an accident – it is something he senses that she will end up praying for.

'All you can do, Zarifa, I keep saying it – is to be here for her.'

'I will, I will – but it will be a long time before she crosses our door – I burned her ears with what I said to her, and his also.'

Not so long till you see her, Khalil thinks, not long at all – for surely even an errant daughter will attend her father's funeral?

'One more thing, Zarifa – that night, after leaving O'Driscoll with Sourb, I was driven to Sourb's old place to collect my car – the moon was half up, shining through the tree. A rope swayed in the breeze and another beside it creaked and strained under the American's weight – he had been forgotten in all of this.'

'Why are you talking about him – you weren't inv—'

'I just remembered the relief I felt at having nothing to do with his death, and the sudden switch to despair when I realized that in everyone else's eyes I had been involved – the same way they believed I had been involved with the attempt to kill O'Driscoll. A tacit compliance.'

He takes a beer instead of arrack, a cigar in place of his water pipe. On his way to the garden Zarifa says she will bring him some rice cakes.

He doesn't answer.

26

Khalil wakes first, catches the sun coming up. Knocks on Daoud's door, peeps in, enters on his tiptoes, which he then thinks is absurd, given that his intention is to waken the boy.

Daoud sleeps under a white mosquito net, a net sparsely populated with the remains of dead mosquitoes. His sheets lie crumpled at his feet. He wears nothing except a pair of blue boxers, his tiny testicles visible through the fly, a ladder of brown spots on his shoulders. His features as trouble free as a blue sky. Hair standing on his head. In a boy's eyes Canada is such a long way from Lebanon – but it is for the best. Will he ever say a prayer for an old man from his childhood days? Allah, let the boy grow strong and sturdy, grant him always, above everything else, sound health of mind and body.

'Daoud,' he whispers.

Again.

And again, this time gently shaking his shoulder.

'Khalil!'

Up, wide-eyed.

'Are we late?'

'No, breakfast is ready – hurry.'

'Khalil?'

'Yes?'

'Yesterday—'

'Yesterday.'

'Yesterday I was talking to a Fiji man – he wants to buy a radio for forty dollars but I tell him no – no deal on sales price.'

'And?'

'Was I right?'

'Yes, no discount in a sale.'

'He said I was a little fucker.'

'Point him out if he comes today.'

'What'll you do, Khalil?'

'Sell him his radio for thirty dollars, maybe less.'

Daoud's lower lip falls a little.

'Chin up, Daoud – I'll let him bargain me down to thirty dollars – he'll want it dropped again, so – but next week, when you're in Canada and I'm at home and the shop is closed, his radio will break down. The slightest knock and they're useless.'

'Is that the right—'

'Being nice to a customer, Daoud, and giving him what he wants – something for a cheap price – and the quality to match.'

'But Khalil, he should be kicked out of the shop for calling me names.'

'Ah, child, why upset yourself, the Fijian and the customers? No. You never lose your temper with a customer – not if you want his money – and a businessman needs money.'

Daoud is less than satisfied with Khalil's reasoning.

'I better get dressed, Khalil.'

'Good boy – remember, everything you do now will affect everything you do in the future – the shadows of the things you do can follow you for years.'

'Uncle Khalil – what do you mean?'

Khalil smiles, *Uncle*, 'You'll know in time.'

The boy eats a boiled egg and asks for another but they have no more. He asks about Cutie, who will mind her when he's gone, and Khalil buries a smile – there's a problem solved of its own accord. The boy isn't stupid, he knows it is not feasible to bring the cat to Canada.

'I'll be delighted to take care of her – every time I look at her I will wonder how my old worker is doing in Canada.'

'I don't mind leaving Cutie with you and Zarifa – you're kind people. Mamma says you're the kindest people she has ever known.'

Khalil's heart swells a little.

Ah, perhaps Allah will hear some prayers said for my soul after all.

'I think she's right.'

'That is kind of you to say, Daoud.'

'It's only true.'

They leave for the shop at eight. A dull and dour day with high prospects of remaining that way for its duration. Grey and sulking skies. Not a summer's day – a day out of season. Khalil thinks how weather patterns are changing all over the world. In 1991, three years ago, he spent a week in Tibnin with his cousin, Hassan Tayab.

The village of Tibnin is about 18 km from the coastal road, situated high in the hills under the higher position of the SLA's Charlie Compound whose Merkava tanks frequently shell the surrounding hamlets of Haddatha, Al Jurn, As Sultaniyah, Brashit and Tibnin itself. Hassan and his family lived under the crusader castle. A sombre hilltop fortress with four stout corner turrets – a winding path led to an arched entrance that Khalil remembered walking with his father. Hassan, who died the following year in a car accident, told him that the great Saladin laid siege to the castle and allowed the last surviving thirteen crusader knights to leave without being harmed. Sparing their lives because the French had earlier showed mercy to the Muslims in the village. Castle Toron – the castle of the turrets – Khalil watched as snowflakes began to drift across the window, the first within living memory, falling heavier and heavier, blanketing the ground, the honey coloured castle walls, the roads, the wadis, their rocks jutting out like sharp grey tongues. The bitter cold, the soft nights, the stealth of the snow as it fell for days, the slush two weeks later, when he was at home, the floods Hassan rang to tell him about, that destroyed their house and stank to the high heavens, because the disused village water hole had burst its banks – algae and centuries old shit and piss – probably crusader shit.

Khalil sent him some money, some carpets, some furniture. Not as much as he would have liked to give but enough to start him off, to offer him and his family some cheer.

Snow. The feel of it on his face, like cold fingertips – the things you think you forget, the way they come back. The stars shining above the castle's uneven line, the crunch of snow under his feet as he walked Zarifa home from a party in the village's Christian sector that was reached by a long, winding ascent through narrow streets, the descent treacherous in places, so they trod carefully for they were of an age when a slight fall could inflict a lot of pain.

As Khalil parks, Daoud gets out and runs to open the shop door. Stretching a coiled keyring clipped to a belt loop on his denim shorts. Turning the key and giving the door a small shove that only someone acquainted with locking and unlocking the door knows of.

Last night was the first night in years that his shop hadn't got a soul staying in it.

He crosses the threshold, seizes the smell of his shop, its slight mustiness, dampness, and dustiness. Its welcome familiarity – scent of his better days.

Daoud dusts the shelves, eager to be doing something before being told to do it – showing Khalil that he is using his initiative as he has been taught.

Khalil moves behind his desk and opens the stiff drawer at the third attempt. Takes out his Debtors book that Adeeba hasn't touched during his absence, instead recording the name and ID card number against the amount submitted on a spiral bound notebook that Zarifa had left out for him this morning.

Some people will make money out of his shop's closure – it is the way of things – credits and debits. No more asking the MPs to track down this man or that woman for monies owed. No more ordering, invoicing, bargaining, customers – the death of his business.

Ah, well . . .

Still, this is a cost saving operation, is it not? Yes – proceeds to help Daoud on his Canadian way. You've written the money off.

Voice.

It shows how well you've done to be so generous, Khalil.

Yes, it does – I've done well.

Yes, Khalil, in most things you've done well.

Leave me alone, for today.

They come in dribs and drabs – first the early risers, the Nepalese, followed by the Ghanaians, the Irish, the Fijians, a Finn who looks lost and a Pole with calculating eyes, a scout's eyes for his comrades waiting back in barracks.

Everyone loves a bargain.

Some insist on haggling, but Khalil declines many times to individuals and walks away, smiling, a good-humoured quip leaving his lips.

Daoud excels – he has learned – none of the shyness of old, none of the cheekiness – now he smiles and shows his palm to buyers, indicating, 'Feed me, please,' following Khalil's example. The sticky customers he refers to his 'Boss'.

A child matured beyond his years. Then he has seen and heard much in his few years. He sold the Fijian who had ver-bally abused him a radio for $25, making him promise not to tell another person, 'Special price for you only, my friend.'

Thumbs up to Khalil when the happy soldier passed through the door with his radio in a box under his arm.

Zarifa calls in to say that the shop is to close at four – there is a meal being laid on in the Splash Restaurant – courtesy of the Street's traders and a presentation to be made.

'Khalil, you should think of something fitting to say.'

'Was this to be a surprise?' he asks.

'Yes – so act surprised. I had to tell you – I couldn't wait – it's a great honour, Khalil. How many other traders have closed around here without a murmur raised at their passing?'

Khalil smiles, 'Perhaps they are glad to see the back of me?'

Most of the stock is cleared within three hours – hour by hour he drops his prices until the shelves are full of shiny spaces amongst the dust – all that remains are a few broken water pipes, crockery, ornaments, bric-a-brac that he and Daoud place in boxes outside for customers to help themselves to or for the Friday rubbish collection. Done weekly by a Christian called Antoun from Faqra village, a man with a grille voice box in his throat that he presses on to speak. Inside, he turns his eye around the empty shop – Daoud beside him, then leaving to sprinkle the floor with water before sweeping.

'Leave it, Daoud, leave it, boy – our day is done.'

'O.K.'

Khalil walks into the small room, decides to leave the new mattress behind, the trappings of tea and coffee making – if some poor soul wants to wander in he has a ready-made home. It is unlikely – the tin houses along the street are emptying one by one – those remaining, the survivors, will be replaced by concrete buildings with marble façades.

He had half expected to see O'Driscoll or Hennessy today,

but in fact no MPs had been in his shop. A surprising fact – obviously Hennessy had warned them off. In the olden days if such a thing were to happen, the gates of the Unifil camp would be blockaded until the out of bounds sanction was lifted.

He turns the sign to read 'Closed' and gets into his car, Daoud climbing into the passenger seat, saying, 'That's that, Khalil.'

It has been a good day. He snatched rest periods here and there – and besides the work had never felt like work to him, and it hadn't today. How much has he made? A little short of $3,500 – as much as he had reckoned on receiving. He saw them all in the Splash – friends and neighbours – Jesso, Kasni who reminded him about the wedding on Saturday. Khalil express the hope that he would be up to attending. Faces he knew when they were children's faces – friends, acquaintances, kindred spirits – they had come to see him off.

It is true what Kasni says in his speech, repeating himself, this man who kick-starts his sentences with Mmmm, 'Mm, Khalil was the Street's if not the village's Muhktar, its elder statesman, a dispute settler, a generous giver to worthy causes – things he thinks we know nothing about . . .'

A note of worry – near the restaurant's glass doors he sees Aziz in earnest discussion with Daoud. Moments later his finger aims at Dahab, his lips stretched, showing his teeth like a snarling dog protecting its food.

Khalil can't move, trapped in conversation, his eyes motioning Zarifa to investigate.

Zarifa steps between the pair. Aziz steps back, folds his arms, and gesticulates.

'Excuse me,' Khalil says to Tommy the Coffee Man.

Weaves his way between tables and chairs, aware of a silence beginning to drip.

'Aziz, this is neither the time nor the place,' he says.

'Who are you to come between husband and wife – who does your wife think she is to interfere?'

'It's not interfering.'

'Is it not? *She* thinks she's bringing Daoud to a fun park on Saturday – I say she's not. He'll have more fun at the wedding – there's a bouncy castle, a puppet show laid on for the children – this is my son, my business – you know about it but that gives you no right to speak on it – neither of you old people has a right.'

Dahab says, 'My name isn't She – it's Dahab – I lived with you long enough and carried two children for you to have earned some respect.'

Khalil cuts in, 'Dahab, Aziz is right – it's a long drive to a fun park in Beirut when there is one here – let him go. Beirut can wait.'

Dahab's mouth opens but Aziz cuts in, 'And don't heed

the boy when he says he would sooner go to Beirut – put some discipline on him.'

'Like we did to our other boy, you mean?'

Aziz reaches for her but Kasni and Jesso pull him away – Kasni reprimanding him.

Under the candy-striped awning Aziz struggles, crooking his leg around a table leg.

'I will call for him on Saturday! Dahab, have him ready for me.'

'You bastard! We'll be in Beirut taking a flight away from you,' Dahab says, her hand leaving her throat to cap her words – her eyes wide and surprised at her stupidity.

Aziz out of view, on the street, screams that he will kill her, shoot her dead – his new wife running to join him, knocking over a flowerpot in her haste, the earth freshly watered, petals broken from the sunflower, like small yellow wings plucked from a canary.

Chaos.

A talking point for everyone, Zarifa says, on the journey home – the embarrassment!

Dahab bites her thumbnail. Daoud sobs. Khalil's fingers tight and white on the steering wheel.

Aziz is mad and bad enough to call around this evening and go berserk, take the boy, and run.

At home Khalil calls Tyre Port, querying the time of the next ferry to Paphos or Limassol.

Ten – the ferry calls at both Cypriot stops. They've four hours. Easily make it, if there's room. Another call confirms that there is.

Dahab listens to his plan. The night ferry to Limassol, a cab ride to Larnaca, a flight from there to Montreal. It's all arranged – she might have to book into a hotel for a night before flying out – he recommends the Pegasus.

'It's best to move now, Dahab – you understand? – are you packed? Passports—?'

She nods. A frail woman, weak – Allah, give her the courage, the fibre to toughen things out, for Daoud's sake.

'Zarifa will drive you – as far as Aziz is concerned I will tell him that you have gone to spend some time with Adeeba.'

He arranges the luggage into the boot – the streetlights coming on as he squeezes Daoud's hand.

'The best goodbyes are the quickest ones – mind your mother, mind yourself.'

'Khalil – I want you to have these.'

The boy hands over prayer beads.

'They were Sami's – he gave them to me.'

'Daoud—'

'Take them, please.'

'A fair trade, Daoud – take these beads – they were my father's.'

The beads Khalil's father turned Daoud now turns. The path of beads a prayer way to Heaven, a dispersing of worries, a thing to do when there is nothing else he can do.

They hug. Daoud leans over and rubs Cutie.

Before Zarifa drives away he presses a brown envelope into Dahab's hands, 'This is Daoud's wages – he worked hard for them.'

'Thanks . . .' Dahab says.

'Go, go now.'

He watches the car pull away until it passes the bend. Then, turning for the path he gathers Cutie in his arms and heads indoors.

27

He sits in the darkened kitchen, a frilled green blanket covering his knees. He had spent some time in the garden, sitting by the pond, until the mosquitoes began to bite. He felt strange. Light in himself – could not finger it exactly – there was what? An air of expectancy in his bones – he imagined it was how a soldier felt seconds before a battle was due to commence, those terrible still and silent seconds, when even the birds absent themselves from the skies.

An hour ago he vomited in the downstairs toilet, emptied his lungs, double dosed and a bit on painkillers. Rolled a hashish cigarette and smoked but it did nothing for him.

His nerves left unmassaged.

He closes his eyes, mouth dry and feeling wasted.

Cold, so damn cold.

The house.

He detests its emptiness.

Frightens him.

No Daoud, no Dahab, no Adeeba, no Zarifa – just a kitten for company – a kitten who patrols the garden and will come to the kitchen door meowing when hungry. Zarifa had called to say that Dahab and Daoud were on the ferry. She stayed to see them off. Sad, to see them leaving – she was staying in a hotel tonight. Didn't fancy driving along the coastal road in the dark, passing through the UN check-points, and Charlie Swing Gate might be closed.

Would be closed, he corrected.

He had forgotten about the artificial border. No, she had to stay in Tyre, he told her, had to – go to Tyre Rest House – spoil yourself. Ring me later.

Cold.

O'Driscoll and Hennessy – had they really thought that he was going to lead them to the grave? Or had they acted as though they believed? Wanted to believe? Probably a mix-ture of all three. He had come so close to giving in.

The man is dead now, so Zarifa would have him believe.

Adfal was always the deep sort and had eyes that shut you off at a certain point. He never let people get too close to him.

In the beginning why had he spared O'Driscoll?

Zarifa never said.

He wrung the necks of the insane as though he were

culling substandard chickens. The fox in the asylum hen coop. Or they were helped to fall from a height. She told him.

Why spare the Irishman?

Was it because he pitied him? The rope burns on the neck he could somehow associate with?

Adfal has a villain's history.

Or was it as Adfal had said – the Irishman never caused any trouble, was quiet and didn't, as Zarifa breathed, strain meagre resources? What she meant to say, Khalil is sure, is that he never overburdened his carers, never strummed their nerves. The lost of Lebanon. The truly lost – the ones the war drove mad, the ones the war killed in another way. Would Adfal, in a place of sanctuary, take everything from those who had almost nothing?

O'Driscolls, forgive me.

He decides to retire for the night, but hasn't the energy to move. His legs are as though they don't exist or have become a different entity from the rest of him – have rebelled against his brain's command.

Tired. So tired. He thinks how Zarifa might be lying – Adfal didn't cull humans, mad or sick. Did he look like someone who would be capable of carrying out such horrible deeds?

Silly question, Khalil.

Voice. Go away.

Why say that about her brother? To comfort a dying hus-band? Come, Khalil – why?

I don't know.

Would you like me to tell you?

Do.

To save you talking, to save you spilling a secret – to keep your mouth shut.

He nods. Perhaps. But she had advised him to let O'Driscoll see his father?

A mystery. Brother and sister – close – blood ties – ah.

What had changed her mind? Something Adfal had said?

The pain, when it comes, hits hard and fast, slaps his back against the chair – his eyes bulging, his mouth opened wide in a silent scream.

It is a piercing agony – a knife driven between his ribs, the long serrated blade turning slowly, as though his innards were on a spit, the flame upped.

Wide-opened eyes see nothing.

His ears catch the faintest rustling of trees and a cat's meowing – then these, too, are lost to him.

28

Hennessy drives Jimmy the short haul from the MP camp to Italair. Jake is in a plastic flight kennel, locked in so he doesn't go wild on the heli. His snout and sad eyes visible through the visor.

'He doesn't like flying,' Jimmy says, 'Throws up.'

'Errah, he'll be fine – it's only thirty minutes to Beirut – the Dogface will meet you off the Helipad – he'll take care of Jake when you're in the valley.'

'You've been a great help, Tom, thanks.'

'Don't mention it.'

Jimmy dons the helmet and safety jacket in the waiting room, nods towards the other passengers. On the pad the chopper's engine is kicking over, the blades revolving.

An Italian officer in flying gear calls for attention and lists off safety rules. Jake barks when he finishes, as though on cue.

Aboard, strapped in, the heli lifts from the ground, tips forward and begins to rise, over and out to sea, above the MP billets, above Tom and the cruiser he's parking, straightening for Beirut.

At the chopper terminal Jimmy takes the keys of a cruiser from Sokolowski, and hands Jake over, saying he will be back tonight, that they've a late afternoon flight to catch tomorrow. Outside the airport he pulls into a car park and studies the map left for him on the front passenger seat. Jots down some key places along the route on a pad.

The traffic is light exiting Beirut. He takes to a narrow winding road that brings into view beautiful mountain landscapes, the sun smiling on the snow caps, and villages with red-tiled roofs atop hills or fastened to the sides of mountains. Olive groves, vineyards with leather skinned workers and weary donkeys – the road rising higher and higher until he reaches Bcharre, a red-roofed town dominated by three churches.

He parks in front of the Palace Hotel, getting out to stretch his legs and smoke. Orders a coffee and a dry bread roll in the hotel's lounge, idles through a gratis copy of the *Daily Star*.

He isn't too far away now, a slow drive into the gorge for about 5 km and then a 3 km hike along a trail. The place he is searching for is not too far from Deir Mar Elisha monastery, an old disused church and cells carved into the

299

walls – reached by a stairwell of craggy stone steps, he imagines.

He parks the cruiser on a gravel car park busy with vehicles, taking the short-term visitors' side. The other patch reserved for the occupants of the various Maronite churches in the gorge.

Sets off, carrying a canteen of water, wearing shades and trainers to guard against sharp stones, along the narrow trail.

It's hot. He is not alone, others walk in front and behind, geared up to hike farther into the valley, some 50 km long. He branches away to the left, realizes when he hits the track that he could have taken the cruiser down without too much trouble, using four-wheel drive, but perhaps not without a scratch or two happening.

He strolls past the monastery, admiring and wondering at how people had cut into the sun baked stone, a task that must have taken successive generations to complete.

Rounding a bend the place he is looking for comes into view. It is like a skull carved into the side of a mountain – eyes, nose and mouth reached by twisting and spiralling steps with brown guard rails.

The red jeep parked beside two others he recognizes, the same one he had seen parked outside the hotel in Sidon, the night he followed Khalil.

Jimmy takes a deep breath and begins to ascend.

The mouth is wide, double doors opened, its floor layered

with thick carpets. A generator hums in an adjoining cell, powering the laptop a thin man is tapping away at.

Rubber plants in large round pots circle the large cave. Framed lithographs of Tyre and Sidon fixed to the walls, also some short and skinny rugs. A tiger skin, teeth caught in a snarl, lies in front of an unlit kerosene heater.

The man looks up, speaks in Arabic before switching to French at Jimmy's puzzled expression.

'Try English,' Jimmy says.

'Ah, I was wondering when you would come.'

'Wondering?'

'Yes – you are the Irishman's son, yes?'

'Yes, and who am I talking to?'

'Adfal. Zarifa's brother, Khalil's brother-in-law.'

'What exactly is this place?'

'An asylum.'

'Asylum?'

'Yes. We keep some of our mad locked up in Lebanon.'

'Where is my father buried?'

'You mean Khalil didn't tell you?'

Jimmy sits on a chair turned sideways in front of Adfal's desk.

'We don't bury people when they die here – we cremate.'

'I—'

'I can show you the ash pits in the caves – they are only a walk up the road.'

'You cremate—'

'Take a look around you – bury people here – the only people that are laid to rest in the caves are the Patriarchs – the rest are cremated. It isn't such an unpleasant task, in fact it's rarely carried out these days – we don't have that many people staying here, only the very mad, the dangerously violent.'

'My father?'

'Yes. He was dead when they brought him here. Zarifa rang and asked me if I would help her – I agreed.'

'So, you cremated him?'

'Yes.'

Jimmy gets to his feet.

It's over. Trail cold. Jimmy studies the other's features, but there is no sign of a lie. What there is is a calmness bordering on serenity. Still waters. A sureness, too, of the ground under one's feet.

At least I know Dad was here. Is here. This is where he ended up. I have found out something – yet there remains a test, a pebble that might ripple still waters.

'I can show you where we buried his ashes.' Adfal pauses, rising to his feet, 'We seal the pits after a while, pour concrete over the remains. The monks come by every so often and light candles and say prayers – come, I will show you.'

The other is a slight, graceless man, and gives the appearance of an inner coiled strength. He looks and walks like he had carved the caves out by himself. They leave by the way

Jimmy had entered, walking up a slope to another entrance that smells like a fireplace that hasn't been cleaned out, ever. There are suction fans here and there. The walls black, a series of pits covered with concrete blocks bearing Latin inscriptions.

'These are old ones, from the Middle Ages – your father's – come along, in through here.'

An adjoining opening that reveals more sealed pits.

'Here, I think, almost sure.'

'Almost?'

'Yes, remember many came here over the years with no names, no history.'

'My father had a history.'

'I am sorry, but he had no history – how could he? Who knew him to tell me?'

He chews on his lower lip then continues, 'If I hadn't done as Zarifa asked, then they would have buried him else-where – as it was we were set to cremate two other poor souls, so . . .'

'So, come on in we've a barbecue—'

'No!'

Jimmy recoils. The word as sharp as a slap.

'Please, don't be flippant. It's the truth. I cremated your father. He is dead and in this cave.'

'You have others here, I mean insane people? Alive?'

'Yes – back in the other cave – I'll show you. But these are

303

graves easier to look upon, though don't believe me when I tell you that. Come see.'

Jimmy holds his hand up for Adfal to delay. He drops to his knee and prays, touches the concrete. A flood of memories, a murmured caress of prayer.

Adfal's living dead – dank cells. Iron bars. Grimy padded walls.

Smell of shit and piss.

Laughter, screams and shouts.

Hell – deep in the belly of the mountain.

Christ.

Naked bulbs. Flies. Dance of bluebottles.

'These are our worst cases – there are some less serious. We have others who work with the monks, doing simple little tasks – it is a life for them.'

'Did you remove my father's ring, his silver crucifix?'

The pebble to ripple.

'I have them for you and also his wallet.'

Back in the reception cave, behind his desk, he opens a filing cabinet and removes a brown Manila envelope, emptying the contents onto the desk beside his laptop.

'One Claddagh ring – there's an inscription on the inside.'

'My mother's initials.'

'A wallet, a ten dollar bill, a photograph.'

Jimmy peels over the leather wallet. A photograph of his family at Christmas time.

He swallows hard.

'A chain and cross,' Adfal says.

Jimmy signs for them in a blue ledger and asks over a cigarette and tea why Khalil hadn't taken him here in the first place.

'I expect he feared retribution, but you need to ask him that. The man's a ditherer. We had a woman here who used to call everyone a ditherer,' he smiles, 'You must question Khalil.'

'I will – it'll have to be by phone – I'm leaving Lebanon tomorrow.'

'All I can say is that perhaps he was afraid.'

'Afraid of what?'

'I don't know – Khalil is a strange man, very strange – I mean I expected you here. Zarifa called and said to expect visitors. Why he didn't escort you and instead led you on a wild-goose chase, I have no idea – a strange man. But fear, keep that in mind.'

Adfal walks with Jimmy a little way beyond the monastery, passing a balustraded balcony, where some people are sitting around tables under purple parasols.

'Those are some of the others I mentioned, the ones less afflicted – they are trapped and yet not trapped – they are having their afternoon tea.'

Jimmy shakes Adfal's hand and leaves, taking to the dirt track, feeling happy that he had come away with something and yet also feeling that he had left something more valuable behind.

Adfal sighs, climbs the monastery's steps, goes to a table and beckons a stooped and broken man to his side. Holds his forefinger in front of the other's eyes and draws them to the figure on the climb to Bcharre car park.

'See?'

Mumble.

'That is him, your boy.'

'You are sure, Jimmy, that you don't want to meet him?'

Nods. Mumbles.

Takes a long, lingering look until his son is gone and then turns away, shuffling to his table.